Dream Maker
Charlotte Douglas

TORONTO • NEW YORK • LONDON
AMSTERDAM • PARIS • SYDNEY • HAMBURG
STOCKHOLM • ATHENS • TOKYO • MILAN
MADRID • WARSAW • BUDAPEST • AUCKLAND

ISBN 0-373-22380-3

DREAM MAKER

Copyright © 1996 by Charlotte H. Douglas

This edition published by arrangement with Harlequin Books S.A.

® and TM are trademarks of the publisher. Trademarks indicated with
® are registered in the United States Patent and Trademark Office, the
Canadian Trade Marks Office and in other countries.

Printed in U.S.A.

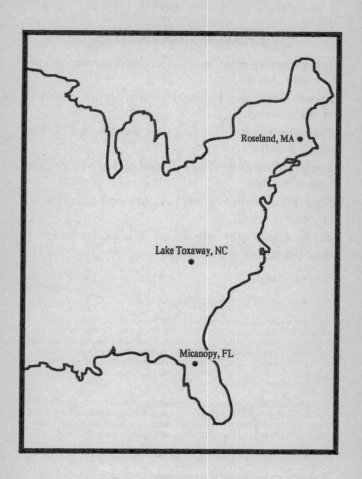

Roseland, MA •

Lake Toxaway, NC
•

Micanopy, FL
•

CAST OF CHARACTERS

Tyler Harris—Her search for independence led her into danger.

Jared Slater—A killer was stalking the woman of his dreams.

Pete Stanwick—The cop was devastated by his wife's murder.

Evelyn Granger—She refused to believe a killer was after her.

Sam Witek—Pete's former partner holds the key to the truth.

Arnie Anderson—He failed in his attempt to stop his father's execution.

Prologue

Jared Slater bolted upright in the darkness with a scream on his lips and blood thundering in his ears. Another dream. Cold mountain air struck the perspiration bathing his bare chest, while his senses reeled from the horror his mind had painted.

He fumbled for the switch on the bedside lamp, but its soft glow brought no comfort. Blackness hovered in his memory, and although the red digits of his radio winked two a.m., he knew sleep would elude him for the rest of the night.

After pulling on sweatpants, a sweatshirt, and thick crew socks, he sprinted down the narrow flight of stairs and flipped on the lights in the great room, the scene of his nightmare. The tranquil setting, with its deep leather chairs, massive fireplace rimmed with mountain stone, and timbered cathedral ceiling, contradicted his dream. Every piece of furniture stood in its place, the door remained securely locked, the ceiling-high windows that overlooked the valley glistened whole, unbroken. And the braided rug in front of the hearth—

He shook his head in an attempt to clear the image of a young woman sprawled there, a bloody gash marring the smooth perfection of her high forehead, and her eyes, the color of mountain mist, staring sightlessly at the ceiling.

Forcing himself across the braided rug where her body had lain in his dream, he removed a pad and pencil from his desk and carried them into the kitchen, where he turned on the coffeemaker before trying to capture the details of the horror that had awakened him. The insidious nightmare coiled like a python in his brain, strangling all thoughts except the visions from his dream.

The woman had seemed familiar—he had experienced an overwhelming affection for her—but awake, he had no idea who she was or why she had been there.

A shudder racked his body. Even with the central furnace pumping warm air into the room, he couldn't shake the chill. He poured steaming coffee into an earthenware mug, carried it to his chair in front of the fireplace, and then touched a match to logs and kindling. In a few minutes, a cheerful blaze crackled and hissed in the stillness.

Pictures hovered in his head of the woman who had died—a small-framed woman in her twenties, with long black hair, gray eyes, a heart-shaped face and a clear complexion. She'd been determined, independent, good-natured, and incredibly beautiful.

"I loved her."

His words echoed back from the high ceiling, and the grief that had seized him in the dream refused to release him. Anguish skewered his heart with a numbing, intimate despair. The woman in the dream hadn't been a stranger he'd never known, would never know; he had *loved* her.

Images from his nightmare replayed in his mind: the beam of sunlight that had turned her hair to glistening jet as she entered the room through the front door, calling him by name; the glimpse of rhododendron blooming on the mountainside; the stack of mail she had sorted before extracting a priority envelope with a look of pleased anticipation; the force and direction of the explosion as it had knocked her off her feet.

Exhausted from reliving the woman's death again and again, Jared drained his cup, padded into the kitchen for a refill, and tossed another log onto the fire. Then he settled into the leather depths of his chair again.

The dreams had begun two years ago. He'd considered the first one merely a creation of his sleeping brain until he read in the newspaper that the woman he'd dreamed about had died. When the second horrible vision visited him in his sleep, he'd worked frantically to identify the woman in order to save her. He had discovered her identity too late. Now, already faced with the death of a third victim, the doom of a fourth woman had been thrust into his consciousness.

Was fate playing some horrible practical joke, showing him the future while denying him the ability to change it?

Or was this latest dream a sign that he could finally make a difference? The woman had been in his house, his living room. To keep her safe, all he had to do was deny her entry. If he couldn't save the others, at least he could save her.

For the first time since awakening from the grisly vision of the woman's death, the tension eased from his muscles. Jared laid his head back against the soft cushion and stared at the flickering flames.

The fire burned low, and bleak predawn light tumbled through the high windows before he finally drifted back to sleep.

Chapter One

Tyler Harris shivered in the freezing wind, tugged her jacket tightly around herself, and paced the pavement of the almost deserted service station. The only other customer, a burly man, turned up the collar of his black leather topcoat and stared at her from beneath the raised hood of a black Blazer, parked in the repair bay. Under the pale sodium lights that had been activated by the storm's encroaching darkness, his lifeless eyes glistened like pools of stagnant water in a face as hard and chiseled as the granite of the surrounding mountains.

With a nervous shudder, she turned from his disturbing scrutiny to the elderly attendant who had just filled her tank. "I'm headed for the Slater place at Lake Toxaway. Is this the right road?"

"Well, missie, it is—and it ain't. Ice storm's blowing in across the mountains. Weather bureau's just issued travelers' advisories." The grizzled old man counted out her change and pointed across the highway. "You could put up at the motel there. It's right clean and not too pricey. That fellow with the Blazer's already reserved his room."

The thought of being snowbound with the Blazer's menacing owner repelled her more than the sleeting rain that stung her cheeks. She slipped into her car and consulted the map folded on the seat. "I'd better get moving. I can reach Lake Toxaway within the hour. If I delay and the roads ice up, I could be stuck here for days."

The attendant's kindly face fell. "Suit yerself."

"Brevard's a lovely town," she said, attempting to salve his disapproval, "but I'm reporting for a new job today, and I don't want to make a bad impression by arriving late."

The attendant moved away, but before she could raise her window, the man with dead eyes appeared beside her car. "You'd better stay away from Slater's place."

She shivered at the threat in his voice. "What do you mean?"

His shrugged his leather-clad shoulders. "People around Slater keep turning up dead."

She forced herself to meet his lifeless gaze. "What people?"

"Good-looking women, like you." He eyed the UNC-Chapel Hill parking sticker on her windshield. "If I were you, I'd turn around now and head back where I came from."

She searched for meaning in his blank expression, but his rough face told her nothing. ''Do you know Jared Slater?''

''I wish to God I didn't.'' The man turned abruptly and paced across the pavement toward the garage without a backward glance.

''Just drive careful, missie,'' the attendant called as she pulled away from the pumps. ''Those mountain curves are treacherous in the best of weather.''

She closed her window against the icy blast and turned up the heater. In an attempt to regenerate her excitement over her new job, she dismissed the stranger as a crank. For all she knew, the man didn't know Slater at all. He looked like the type who would get his jollies from frightening women with his sullen looks and threats.

''A nut case,'' Tyler decided as she pulled back onto the deserted highway. She refused to consider that Jared Slater might be dangerous. That fact would throw a major kink in her well-laid plans.

Only two weeks ago, she had discovered an ad posted in the main staff lounge of the university library.

Wanted immediately—full-time research assistant for freelance writer. Must be willing to relocate to Lake Toxaway, N.C., and occasionally travel. Salary negotiable. Room and board provided.

Jared Slater's name and E-mail address were at the bottom of the ad.

She had completed her research, tracking down every tidbit of information she could glean about Jared Slater before composing a response. She'd almost given up hope of landing the job, when three days ago his acceptance of her application and an irresistible salary offer had arrived in her electronic mailbox.

The position made her dream of independence come true. She welcomed the opportunity to earn her own living and at the same time escape the velvet clutches of her darling, but overprotective, grandmother.

The wind buffeted her car and blasted rain across her path as she headed up the steep grade, lighted only by the high beams of her headlights. Other travelers must have heeded the weather advisory and taken shelter from the sleeting rain, for she passed only a large tractor-trailer truck, easing its way in low gear down the mountain.

While concentrating on the slippery road, she considered what she'd uncovered about the man she would meet within the hour. Jared Slater had become a man of mystery. Born in Virginia to a family that had made their wealth through tobacco, he'd had a brief but stellar career as an investigative journalist in Washington. After recovering from a life-threatening illness, he'd resigned from the *Post* and disappeared into seclusion in the North Carolina mountains. No one seemed to know what he'd been doing since. If he'd been writing freelance, as his ad stated, she could find no trace of his work.

She'd studied the grainy photo that accompanied his last article, completed just after his illness. Wide-set eyes softened the Hollywood ruggedness of his square jaw, patrician nose, and strong brow. Those eyes had reflected a strange, haunted look, possibly the result of his earlier brush with death, but a latent kindness had shone there, too. A good thing, since it would be just the two of them working alone each day in his mountain retreat in the back of beyond.

She pushed aside her niggling doubts and the stranger's bizarre warning and wondered why a trained investigative reporter would need his own researcher and what he was working on, hidden away in the Smokies.

The storm's intensity increased, and by the time she reached the turnoff to Lake Toxaway, her hands were cramped from clutching the steering wheel, as if the force of her grasp would hold her car to the treacherous road. Her head pounded from straining to see the highway through the freezing rain and darkness.

She pulled into the parking lot of a small grocery, the only commercial building in sight, extracted a penlight from her purse, and reviewed the map and directions Jared had sent.

"Why didn't he just say the middle of nowhere?" she grumbled as she threw the car into gear again. She re-entered the deserted highway and searched through the blackness for the church he had specified.

"I hope your directions are good, Jared Slater," she muttered through clenched teeth. "I don't fancy spending the night lost on this mountain in an ice storm."

She found the turnoff at the church and the first and second forks, but when her odometer indicated she'd gone too far since the last fork, she knew she'd missed Slater's driveway. She turned around in front of a summer cottage, shuttered against winter storms, and eased her way back down the road.

A blowing evergreen branch had obstructed Slater's sign on her first pass, but this time she located his driveway and headed up the gravel road, longing for a cup of hot coffee and a roaring fire. In spite of the heat blasting from her defrosters, her windshield iced as the temperature dropped. Water had crystallized on the trees and shrubbery lining the narrow drive. She jumped at the gunshot crack of a limb, broken by the weight of its frozen burden, that scraped the trunk of her car as it fell. Through leafless trees, a building loomed in the darkness on the mountaintop, like a setting for a Gothic horror film. Light from its tall windows glittered dimly through the dangerous storm.

Inching her way forward over the icy road, she focused on the narrow strip ahead, all too aware of the dark ravine on her right. Should her car slide, there was no barrier to prevent a plunge down the mountainside. When she reached the entrance to Slater's house, the cramping in her fingers had spread to every muscle of her body.

She parked in front of the garage doors, left her bags in the car, and, slipping and stumbling, managed to reach the front door without falling. When she banged the massive brass knocker, the howling of the wind muffled its pounding.

Ice coated her jacket and hair, and cold bit into her bones while she waited. Just as her teeth began rattling, the door swung open, and Jared Slater glowered down at her. Shocked recognition flashed in his eyes, which seemed odd, since she'd never met him.

"Good God, woman, are you lost?" He hesitated, then opened the door wider and with an air of reluctance pulled her inside.

"I w-was, but th-then I—" Her chattering teeth made her words incomprehensible.

After he stripped her sodden coat from her shoulders, she maneuvered close to the blazing fire, the only source of light in the dim, cavernous room.

"Anyone else with you?" he asked.

Afraid to trust her voice, she shook her head and stretched her frozen hands toward the fireplace, conscious of her isolation on the mountaintop with a man she knew nothing more about than the few facts she'd gleaned from her research—and a stranger's dire warning.

His movements sounded behind her, but she didn't shift her gaze from the mesmerizing, flickering flames. The sight of his disapproving eyes had only increased her uneasiness. Slowly warmth returned to her hands

and feet, and her teeth no longer clacked like casta-
nets.

"You can't travel back down the mountain in this
weather." His rough baritone blended with the
screaming wind that buffeted the windows. She
jumped when he grasped her elbow, then flushed with
embarrassment at her nervousness as he guided her
into a deep chair that enfolded her like an embrace.

"Didn't you hear the travelers' warnings?" Disapproval colored his words. "What are you doing up
here in this godforsaken weather?"

She tore her gaze from the flames and forced herself to study Jared Slater. "Looking for you."

His deep brown eyes assumed a hooded look and his
jaw hardened. In the fire's dancing light, his towering
presence and stern expression emanated a strong sense
of menace. Prickles of uneasiness crept along her skin.
Maybe the stranger at the gas station hadn't been a nut
case after all, because the man before her, with his
haunted eyes and lips set in a tight, ominous line,
looked capable of mayhem.

He sat opposite her and leaned forward, clasping
the long fingers of his strong hands between his knees.
"*Why* are you looking for me?"

Chills flittered along her spine from the roughness
of his tone. Why had he offered her a job, then acted
as if he didn't know why she was there? Anger dis-
persed her shivers.

"I'm reporting for work. I'm Tyler Harris."

JARED FELL BACK in his chair. The knowledge that *she* was Tyler Harris hit him like a falling boulder. "I'm sorry, Ms. Harris, but the position is filled."

The lie rolled easily off his tongue. He would lie—and more—to be rid of her, the victim in his latest disturbing dream, who had appeared just as he'd known she eventually would.

But the fact that she was Tyler Harris stunned him. He'd hired Harris as his research assistant, assuming Tyler to be a man, specifically to avoid this situation. But fate had backfired on him again, proving that his nightmares and the deaths of the women in his dreams would always come true.

Her gray eyes clouded, and with a trembling hand, she rummaged in the depths of her black leather purse and withdrew a folded paper. "I don't understand. I have your letter of acceptance right here."

He would have a tough time getting rid of her, but he had no choice. "Yes, well, there's been a terrible mistake—"

"Mistake? You offered me the job, I accepted, and I'm reporting to work as instructed." Her wide, innocent stare pierced his conscience.

He shifted his weight uneasily beneath her scrutiny and breathed deeply, stalling for time. "The offer was a mistake. I can't hire you."

"Can't—or won't?"

"What difference does it make? You can't have the job." Knowing he was acting like a cad lent a harsh edge to his voice.

She stood and paced before the fire, chafing her arms as if to warm them, but the heat of her indignation reached all the way across the room.

"I gave up my apartment and my previous job to come here, moved across the state—and drove through an ice storm so I wouldn't report late. Now you tell me the job is filled. You'll have to do better than that."

Regret washed through him. She surpassed the promise of her résumé. In addition to outstanding academic qualifications, Tyler Harris possessed the spark needed to tackle the puzzles confronting him.

But hiring her would mean her death.

He steeled himself against her anger. "You may be qualified for the job, but I chose you because I thought Tyler Harris was a man."

Her arms dropped to her sides, her hands balled into fists, and an angry flush darkened her face. "You wanted a research assistant. Male or female, what difference does it make?"

Nothing. Everything.

He focused on the fire, avoiding the pleasant spectacle of her glowing cheeks, the tendrils of black hair clinging damply to the porcelain skin of her forehead, the rosy softness of her lips. "Neither your acceptance letter nor your application gave any indication you're a woman. Was that intentional?"

"Maybe it would have been, thirty years ago—" sarcasm laced her voice " —but we're out of the Dark Ages now. Sexual discrimination is against the law."

He sighed. "You're right, but I still can't hire you."

Her eyes blazed like burnished pewter. "Is there something about this job that requires a man?"

Jared remembered his nightmare, but he couldn't admit he refused to hire her because of a bad dream. "Yes, the job's too dangerous. You could get hurt."

"Doing research?"

He sensed her sudden stillness and glanced up to find her scrutinizing him. Her face spoke volumes, informing him she knew he lied.

He levered himself out of his chair, crossed to the open kitchen, and filled the coffeemaker with water. Her footsteps followed, and while he measured grounds into the basket, her stare stabbed between his shoulder blades. Tension crackled like electricity in the confines of the small kitchen, and after flipping the switch to begin the brewing cycle, he turned to confront her.

She didn't retreat from his stare. Her eyes widened, and the soft wings of dark eyebrows lifted above them. "Are you afraid to work with a woman?"

He burst out laughing. "Not at all."

"Then what is it?"

"I told you, there's risk involved."

"What kind of risk?" Her expression mirrored her doubt.

"You could be killed."

Alarm flitted across her lovely features before she straightened her shoulders and laughed. "By what, a falling reference book? I'm a researcher, for Pete's sake."

He couldn't tell her the truth. No one knew the whole truth, and he had no intention of telling all to anyone except his research assistant—and then, only if he was convinced the man could be trusted.

The heady floral scent of her perfume blended with the aroma of coffee brewing, provoking his senses. She refused to believe she was in danger, so he would try another tack that might seem more plausible.

"Okay, I confess. We're miles from the nearest house, and people around here are pretty conservative. I don't want any scandal created by working with a female assistant."

Her eyes narrowed. "Lake Toxaway's a summer-resort town with a seasonal population. Most don't care who does what, as long as they're not affected."

Persistence might be an excellent quality in a researcher, but in someone he was trying to get rid of, it was a royal pain. "Then let's just say I don't like women, don't want one hanging around, and let it go at that," he lied.

He pulled a mug from the cabinet and slammed it onto the counter. Damn the woman. If an ice storm wasn't raging, he would show her the door and be done with her.

"No, I won't let it go. You promised me this job, and I drove all the way across the state to take it. If you have a problem with that, Mr. Misogynist, you'd better swallow it or I'll put the Equal Employment Opportunity Commission on your case so fast, you won't know what hit you."

His admiration of her gutsy stance dissolved into alarm. A federal investigation was the last thing he needed. He couldn't allow anyone to stop him from doing what had to be done. And how could he explain the real reason he couldn't hire her? No one would believe him.

The steely glint in her eyes, the jut of her jaw and the determined set of her shoulders convinced him Tyler Harris didn't make idle threats. He would have to find some way to placate her without giving her the job.

Tyler turned on her heel, marched back to her chair in front of the fire, and sank into it. She grasped the leather armrests to hide the trembling in her hands while she attempted to gauge whether he was serious about the danger or just using it as an excuse.

She'd made the break she'd needed from Gran and Chapel Hill. If she crawled back now, jobless and homeless, asking Gran for a place to stay until she found work, she would be paraded before an unending stream of incredibly bland and boring young men—the blue-blooded, spineless type Gran wanted her to marry. If Gran had her way, Tyler would spend the rest of her days raising well-mannered children and prize roses and giving insipid bridge parties, all from Gran's antebellum home in Chapel Hill—and from under Gran's thumb.

But at least you would be alive.

A quiver of anxiety shook her as she considered her enigmatic host. As much as she wanted the job and its very generous pay, she had to consider her safety. She thought longingly of the snug little motel in the valley. She could spend the night there, then check with the local authorities to learn more about Slater before pressing him to hire her—or giving up and returning home.

She rose to her feet. "Maybe we should talk about this tomorrow. I'll come back—"

"The roads are too treacherous. You'll never make it down the mountain. Let me pour you some coffee. Then we'll talk."

She wondered if he'd had a change of heart. The tension in the room had eased once she'd threatened to call in the EEOC. Had he thrown in the towel, knowing his statement about not liking women would be just cause for a lawsuit? Or was he only biding his time until the storm ended so he could send her on her way?

A blast of wind struck the house, rattling the windows and doors. The lights flickered, and Jared disappeared into a room off the kitchen. When he returned a few minutes later, he carried two Coleman lanterns and a handful of candles. After depositing them on the table in front of the sofa, he took brass candlesticks from the mantel and placed the candles in them.

"If the ice continues," he said, "the weight of frozen branches will break the power lines. I'll fix some dinner while we still have electricity."

Without waiting for her response, he returned to the galley kitchen and began removing items from the refrigerator, placing them on the counter that separated the kitchen from the living room.

Silence thundered in the room. If they were to be stuck together until the storm passed, she would hold her tongue about the job. If he really was dangerous, as the stranger had warned, she didn't want to antagonize him. She left her comfortable chair and perched on a high stool extracted from beneath the counter's overhang.

He regarded her with a tentative smile, as if the expression was foreign to his face. Maybe he wasn't the ogre he pretended, but she couldn't be certain. She would wait for the wind to drop, then she would leave, but in the meantime, she would play along. She just hoped she was doing the right thing. The job had sounded so wonderful that perhaps she'd been too hasty in her response.

"May I help?" she asked.

He shook his head. "It's a simple meal—just spaghetti and salad."

The green flecks in his brown eyes matched the jade of his cable-knit sweater. He pushed its sleeves toward his elbows, and the corded muscles of his tanned forearms bulged as his long fingers coaxed the cork from a bottle of Chianti classico. Strong hands, strong enough to— She thrust the gruesome thought away. She would have to keep her wits to determine the best time to leave.

He poured a generous amount of Chianti into two wineglasses and handed her one.

"Cheers." The wine blossomed on her tongue and warmed her going down.

Jared's expression sobered as he touched his glass to hers. "Long life."

Another blast of howling wind rocked the house, and she shuddered, wondering if her uneasiness came from the storm or from the strange look in Jared Slater's eyes.

He pulled a chopping board from beneath the counter and began slicing vegetables for a salad, displaying his skill with a chef's knife.

The sight of the gleaming blade reinforced her memory of the stranger's remark that pretty women who spent time around Jared turned up dead. Her nervousness deepened. "Did you mean what you said about not liking women?"

He paused from slicing celery into julienne strips. The silver blade of the huge knife glinted ominously in the firelight. "I meant what I said about not wanting a female research assistant."

"I was speaking in generalities," she said with a jittery laugh.

"Then, generally speaking, some of my best friends were women."

Were. Had he purposely used the past tense? She'd read in a Richmond gossip column about Jared's withdrawal to his mountain retreat after his release from hospital. Maybe he'd abandoned his friends en-

tirely. But if so, why? Or even worse, maybe his female friends were *dead*.

The man was a seething bundle of contradictions.
He'd advertised, specifying an immediate need for a
research assistant, but then had rejected her, even
though she was on the spot and ready to work, because he didn't want a woman around. Yet his demeanor, aside from not wanting to hire her, had been
considerate, almost friendly—once she'd threatened
to file discrimination charges. The man was hiding
something, and her grandmother's warning about
working for a stranger rang in her mind once more.

Gran. She'd be worried sick about her granddaughter traveling in the storm. Tyler had declared her
independence by moving away from the only home
she'd known since her parents' plane crash twelve
years before, but that independence didn't include
thoughtlessness toward the old woman who loved her.

"Mind if I use your phone?" she asked. "I want to
let my grandmother know I'm safe."

Jared pointed with the knife. "Top of the stairs.
While you're making the call, I'll pull your car into the
garage and bring in your luggage. You can stay until
the roads clear."

She would be leaving long before bedtime, but for
now she would do as he asked. She handed him her
keys, then climbed the steep stairs to the loft. Opposite the half wall that overlooked the great room,
French doors provided a panoramic view of the valley and lake below. Snow swirled in eddies across the

balcony, sifting over glittering ice that coated the balustrade and wooden decking.

She circled the bed to a small nightstand that held the telephone and switched on the bedside light. Next to the phone, bold, scrawling words caught her eye. And then, with horror, she found herself reading a description of a woman's murder in graphic detail. Beneath the legal pad, she discovered a folder of glossy black-and-white photos of two murdered women. Newspaper clippings gave their names and the places of their deaths and stated they'd been shot, but did not identify their killer.

The hair on the back of her neck stood on end. Were these women the ones the stranger had meant?

Get a hold of yourself. Jared was a writer. He could be working on an article or maybe even a true-crime novel. She shoved the pad and folder aside, reined in her galloping imagination, and dialed Gran's number.

"Thank God you called," her grandmother drawled in her soft Southern voice. "I've been frantic with worry."

She pictured her grandmother, patting her smooth gray curls with manicured fingers. Gran was probably still dressed in the lilac suede suit she'd worn that morning to the garden club. Tyler anticipated a wave of homesickness, but experienced only a strong affection for the woman who had raised her.

"I'm fine, Gran. Arrived safe and sound before the storm set in. I can't talk but a minute—dinner's almost ready—but I'll call again next week. We may lose phone lines that long because of the ice.''

''And what about this Jared Slater?''

''He's different from what I expected.'' Tyler grimaced at the understatement. No need to frighten Gran.

She chatted for a moment, then hung up the phone and studied the bedroom, looking for some clue to her host's personality, but the sparsely furnished loft, with its wide bed covered in a muted plaid spread, and Shaker chair, revealed little. A wall of doors concealed closets on one side, and opposite them a door opened into a bathroom. Utilitarian but comfortable, the room told her nothing about Jared Slater's character.

She stood at the French doors and watched snow mounding on the balcony. Unless it stopped soon, she would be stuck on the mountain overnight. Time enough to convince Jared to give her the job. Or time enough to be in mortal danger if he really was dangerous, as the stranger had implied.

She turned from the window and bumped into Jared. Jerking aside, she clutched her pounding heart. ''I didn't hear you come up.''

He gazed past her over the valley below. ''Beautiful, isn't it? Peaceful. As if there isn't a trouble anywhere in the world.''

She bit back her reply. *She* had a full load of trouble, wondering when the storm would end and how she could make her escape.

Jared stretched and rolled his head on his shoulders as if awakening from sleep. "I'll show you your room and where to wash up before dinner."

She followed him downstairs into a narrow hallway leading off the great room. His broad shoulders filled the passageway, but for a big man, he moved with appealing grace. Still, he was big enough to overpower an unarmed female. She gave herself a mental shake. If it hadn't been for the crazy man's warning at the service station, she would have considered Jared's size a turn-on, not a threat.

The first door he opened led to a gleaming bathroom. The next revealed a bedroom with twin beds covered in cheerful red chenille spreads. Plaid draperies were drawn against the cold. Her suitcases and laptop computer, a going-away present from Gran, lay on one of the beds.

"Dinner's ready when you are. I'll leave you to unpack." He headed back up the narrow hall toward the kitchen.

No need to unpack. After seeing the pictures in his room, she was fairly sure she no longer wanted the job. She would only be there until the storm ended, which she hoped would be within a few hours. With relief she noted a key in the lock of the bedroom door. At least, if she had to spend the night, she could sleep feeling safe.

In the bathroom, she splashed cold water on her face and stared at her reflection. Her thoughts were as tangled as her hair.

"Tyler Harris, what have you gotten yourself into?"

The woman in the mirror stared back, silent. She knew a loaded question when she heard one.

After taming her hair, she returned to the great room but paused in the doorway, taking in the change in the room. Jared had moved the coffee table in front of the fire and flanked it with two large cushions. Covered with a checkered cloth and centered with brass candlesticks, the table was set for two.

"Pull up a pillow," he said. "I'll bring the food."

She sat cross-legged at the table as Jared placed salad, breadsticks, and a steaming bowl of spaghetti in front of her. He smiled with a grin that cocked one corner of his mouth.

As if on cue, the wind slammed against the house in a brutal gust. The kitchen lights winked and went out, leaving only the feeble glow from the fire, flickering candles, and the mysterious glitter in Jared Slater's eyes to illuminate the room.

THE STRANGER BENT his shoulder into the wind and trudged through the snowdrifts toward the lights that were barely visible ahead. Stupid Southerners. They acted as if a little weather was excuse to shut down everything, but it wouldn't stop him. The Blazer's four-wheel drive had brought him easily to the foot of Slater's driveway, and his snowshoes would take him the rest of the way.

He could reach the house, kill Slater, and disappear. The snow would cover his tracks long before anyone discovered the body on the mountaintop. The cold bit through his leather coat, but the fire of revenge in his belly kept him warm as he climbed the hill and maneuvered toward the lighted window.

Two women had already died and Slater knew too much. The man had to be stopped. The bulk of the stranger's magnum revolver lay heavy against his chest. He had shot and killed before, but that, too, had been a necessity. Only with Slater's death would the killing cease.

He hid in the shadows beneath the eaves, out of the brunt of the north wind, and observed the cozy scene before the flickering fire where the couple sat, enjoying a meal and sipping wine like lovers. The sight of food briefly resurrected his appetite, but he ignored his cravings. Time enough to eat when the job was finished. In the meantime, he would feast on revenge, the dish best served cold.

So, this was a girlfriend of Slater's. With a keen eye, he observed the look on Slater's face as he studied his dinner companion, whose head was bowed over her plate. Yes, Slater was a lovestruck fool. Pain welled in the stranger's heart—stabbing, twisting, making him want to howl with the wind in his agony and rage.

Maybe killing was too good for Slater. Maybe Slater should suffer—suffer as he'd been made to suffer by Slater's actions. And what better way to inflict pain on

Slater than to make him witness the death of a woman he loved?

The stranger yanked off his right glove with his teeth, slid the pistol from its holster, and aimed. Damn. No matter how he aimed the gun through the only uncovered window, the woman was aligned with Slater. If his shot killed them both at once, his purpose was foiled. But he was a patient man. The woman had to move away, and then he would kill her. Maybe he would even wait for another day. Either way, Slater would grieve before he, too, died.

The stranger leaned against the building, tucked his hand, still holding the pistol, inside his coat, and waited.

Chapter Two

Jared poured coffee into a thermos and added wood to the fire before settling opposite Tyler. "I'm surprised the lines held this long. Luckily, I have a battery-powered radio to track the progress of the storm."

He reached behind him to a shelf beside the sofa and flipped a switch. As he replenished her wineglass, an old Simon and Garfunkel ballad filled the room.

"The atmosphere here may not be five-star," he said with a wry grin, "but it ain't bad."

Tyler graced him with a nervous smile, twirled spaghetti onto her fork, and took a bite. Her eyebrows lifted in approval. "You make great spaghetti."

They ate in a silence broken only by the screeching wind, the hiss and crackle of pine logs on the fire, and the smooth sounds of golden oldies. A weather report roused Jared from his contemplation of the woman across the table.

"Travelers' warnings are still in effect," the announcer drawled. "Looks like we're going to be caught in this unseasonal May weather for a while, folks. Power crews are repairing lines, but for some remote areas, power may be out for several days." The folksy announcer broadcast news of the devastating weather as calmly as if plugging a Sunday-school picnic.

"Several days—damn!" Jared tossed his napkin on the table and leaned back against the sofa.

Tyler flinched at his outburst, then flashed him a wobbly smile. "That anxious to get rid of me, are you?"

That, too, but he couldn't say it. "I'm thinking of several days without computers and modems."

"Are you on some kind of deadline?"

His stomach clenched. He had a deadline, all right, in the most literal sense of the word. Several days without access to the public records and resources he needed. Several days before he could hire another assistant. And God only knew how many days before that assistant could report for work. Several days. Less time than that had meant the difference between life and death for Mary Stanwick. He couldn't afford such a delay again.

Tyler viewed the turmoil scudding like storm clouds across the sharp angles of his face. "Is it the murder story?"

"What do you know about that?" His voice lashed at her with all the fury of the wind beating against the timbers of the house. Anger glazed his eyes.

A flush crept up her cheeks. "I couldn't help seeing the notes you left by the telephone."

He leaned forward, drilling her with his scrutiny. "Tell me about yourself. How'd you get a name like Tyler? And why did you choose library science as a career?"

His abrupt reaction piqued her curiosity, and in spite of his obvious reluctance to discuss his work, she refused to change the subject. "I thought all writers liked to talk about their work."

"I can't talk about it." His words hung lifeless in the cooling air, wrung dry of all emotion as he drained his wineglass with a gulp.

"I'm sure what you're doing is much more interesting than the story of my life." She paused, waiting for him to volunteer information, but he sat stone-faced and silent, staring at her with eyes as deep, brown, and unfathomable as the French Broad River. A quiver of fear caused her hands to shake, and she set down her unsteady glass and clutched her napkin in her lap to hide her trembling. Maybe he couldn't talk about his writing because there *was* no book. Maybe his gruesome notes were something else altogether.

She retreated to the safety of answering his questions. "Tyler was my mother's maiden name."

He relaxed visibly at her change of subject. "Having a man's name must cause you problems."

"Only an abundance of junk mail addressed to Mr. Harris or Dear Sir. Until now. You're the biggest obstacle I've encountered because of it."

"I'd say our inconvenience is mutual." He rose to his feet with uncommon ease for such a large man and gathered dishes from the table. "I'll wash these while the water's still hot."

Tyler scrambled to her feet, picked up her plate and glass, and followed him into the kitchen.

"The fireplace knocks the chill off most of the year, but with temperatures like they're predicting, it'll cool fast without electric heat." His chilly gaze raked her from head to foot before he ran water into the sink, added detergent, and plunged the dirty dishes into the suds. "Hope you have some warm clothes in those suitcases."

"Of course, I do." Cold air nipped through the thin silk of her blouse as she cleared the remaining dishes and carried them in to be washed. "I'll dry."

He extracted a clean dish towel from a nearby drawer and tossed it to her. "You didn't answer my other question, about why you chose your career."

"Why should I? You didn't answer mine." She shivered at her own recklessness, then picked up a dripping plate and rubbed it furiously. Jared's refusal to hire her, his secretiveness about his work, the stranger's warning, and the nasty weather gnawed at her nerves.

"Touché, Ms. Harris." An expansive grin softened the stony contours of his square jaw. "You certainly contradict the stereotype."

In spite of everything, she liked him when he smiled. When he didn't, he frightened her. "What stereotype?"

"The mousy librarian in a drab brown dress, sensible shoes, hair pulled back in a tight bun, and thick glasses."

She struggled to keep her tone light. "If I conform to that image, can I have the job?"

He stared at the woman beside him. Even a drab brown dress wouldn't conceal the soft curves of her hips so enticingly encased in gray tailored slacks or the alluring thrust of her small breasts against the shell-pink fabric of her blouse. He doubted that even the tightest bun would tame the rebellious ebony curls, and glasses would frame those intriguing gray eyes like a work of priceless art.

She squirmed under his inspection. "Sorry. I shouldn't have mentioned the job," she said.

He squelched his dangerous thoughts. "You'd better put on warmer clothes. If you get chilled, it may be days before you warm up again. I'll finish here."

When Tyler returned, she'd covered her silk blouse with a knitted burgundy pullover and replaced her low-heeled pumps with thick socks and running shoes. She folded her legs beneath her in the corner of the sofa nearest the fire and stretched her hands toward its warmth. Desire washed over Jared in a torrent, and again he thrust the feelings away.

"Humor me." His voice sounded smooth and even, devoid of the turmoil seething within him. "Why did you become a librarian?"

She stared at the fire, avoiding his gaze. "My parents died when I was twelve and my grandmother took me in. I was her only living relative, so her possessiveness was understandable. She rarely allowed me out of her sight, but I had free run of both the public and university libraries.''

''You grew up in Chapel Hill?''

She nodded. ''That's where Gran lives. Because of her overprotectiveness, I spent a lot of hours reading, escaping into books. Learning new things fascinated me. Becoming a librarian seemed the logical extension of my childhood passion.''

Her eyes sparkled with enthusiasm, exhibiting none of the artificial guile of women he'd known in Richmond nor the tough sophistication of his female counterparts in Washington.

''What about you?'' she asked. ''Why journalism instead of the Slater Tobacco Company?''

So, she'd researched him. He settled back in his chair. ''I had intended to go into the family business, even started college in business administration, but working on the school paper convinced me to switch to journalism. I learned I had a nose for news.''

''Sounds exciting—and researching for stories is not altogether different from what I do.''

She shuddered with cold, and he retrieved an afghan from the back of the sofa and draped it over her knees. When she looked up and thanked him, her face was only inches from his. He caught the subtle fragrance of her perfume and the scent of sunshine in her hair. Reluctantly, he returned to his chair opposite her.

"Journalism taught me a whole new way of looking at the world. Until I learned investigative techniques, I'd accepted the tobacco industry's standard line—that no proof links cigarettes with cancer and heart disease. It's an opinion still held by everyone in my family except me. After I'd gathered my own information and studied it carefully, I could never work for my father. It would be like selling death."

"Must make things tough for you at family gatherings."

"No problem—I don't go."

Her sympathetic smile caught at his heart. It had been too long since he'd had someone to talk to, to understand him; but for now, he couldn't afford the luxury. Not with this woman.

Tyler watched as he raked his fingers through his thick, dark hair. His expression hardened once more, and reflected firelight danced in his eyes. So Jared had shut himself off, not only from his friends, but his family, too. But why? She wanted this job in the worst way, but alarm bells in the back of her mind warned there was much more to Jared Slater than even her painstaking research had revealed, and that something more could be dangerous.

She opened the thermos, poured hot coffee into a mug, and handed it across the table to him. When his fingers brushed hers, a shock raced up her arm, and she jerked away.

"Sorry. Static electricity," he explained.

She retreated into the corner of the sofa, tucking the afghan more firmly around her knees. The heat from the fire warmed her, and in spite of the coffee she'd drunk, she felt drowsy and slightly woozy from wine.

Relaxed, she blurted out the first question that entered her head. "What happened to you two years ago?"

His strong fingers dwarfed the mug as he sipped his coffee. "If you ever want to be a successful journalist, you'll have to make your questions more specific."

"I read you were ill and gave up your job at the *Post*."

"Was it only two years ago? It seems like a hundred." His eyes clouded with pain, and he sat unmoving, as if lost in thought. Again, a gamut of emotions flitted across his face before his eyes focused on her once more. "It's a long story."

"I'm not going anywhere soon. I have all the time in the world."

His head jerked back as if she'd slapped him. "All our days are numbered, Tyler."

She fidgeted, shaken by the veiled threat, uncomfortable under his somber gaze. "Will it take longer than a few hours?"

"What?"

"To tell me what happened to you."

Disregarding her question, he stirred the ashes of the dwindling fire and heaped on more logs. Uncomfortable silence swelled between them, growing and menacing. She couldn't spend the night here. She would have to chance driving down the mountain, even if the storm hadn't abated.

She shifted her gaze to the wall of windows. A hulking black figure dusted with snow stared back at her. She screamed.

Jared whirled from the fireplace, temporarily blocking her view. "What the hell?"

Unable to speak, she pointed past him to the window, but when he moved toward it and out of her way, only a vast expanse of white filled her vision.

"Someone was out there!" she insisted.

He stepped closer to the window, peering out into the whiteness. "There's no one. You must have seen the shadow of a blowing branch, or a reflection from inside the room. Besides, only a maniac would be out in this weather."

Her nerves had unraveled to the point where she could no longer trust her own senses. She *had* seen something, but had her hyperactive imagination twisted a simple shadow or reflection into a looming figure? One thing was certain. She couldn't remain another minute on the mountaintop with Jared Slater and her suspicions. Even if her host was harmless, her own uneasiness would drive her stark, staring mad.

She tossed aside the afghan, retreated to the bedroom, and returned with her bags in hand and her computer carrier slung over her shoulder. She dumped the load beside the door and tugged on her jacket. "Storm or no storm, I can't stay here."

When she reached for the doorknob, Jared blocked her way. "Are you crazy? You can't drive in this weather."

She picked up her bags again. "If I drive slowly, I'll be all right. Now, please, get out of my way."

"Tyler." The sound of her name on his lips caressed her ears. "I feel bad enough about not hiring you, but I couldn't live with myself if you drove your car into the ravine just to escape my poor hospitality."

She hardened her heart against the warmth that coursed through her at his nearness and reminded herself that she was possibly in danger. "I can't stay here."

He clasped her by the shoulders and stared into her eyes, as if searching for something. "You're afraid of me, aren't you?"

She dropped her gaze but did not reply.

He grasped her chin in gentle fingers and tilted her head until her eyes met his once more. "I promise you, Tyler Harris, I am *not* a dangerous man."

Unable to avoid his eyes, she met the full intensity of his gaze, filled with warmth and an unmistakable pain—and she believed him. She had not a single rational motive for doing so, except the affirmation in her heart as she faced him and felt the heat of his fingers against her chin.

For a split second, she closed her eyes and considered her options. She could plunge into the storm, where a faceless figure lurked and an icy road could mean her death, or she could stay the night with Jared Slater, enigmatic, troubled and frustrating, and possibly as dangerous as the perils that awaited outside.

Some choice.

Her only recourse was to listen to her instincts, and they told her to wait. She hoped to God they were right.

"I'll stay." She dropped her bags and set her computer on a shelf by the door. "But only until the storm eases."

Jared removed a down-filled parka from a peg beside the door, shrugged into it and pulled gloves from the pockets. "We'll need more wood before the night is over."

Uneasy with her compromise, she couldn't decide which was least frightening—braving the elements or remaining inside alone. The elements won. "I'll help. Two can carry twice as much."

He opened his mouth as if to protest, but said nothing and opened the door to the arctic blast. The force of the gust almost knocked her off her feet, and she had to put her head down and turn her shoulder into the wind to make forward progress. Sleet stung her cheeks and eyes, and the screeching wind made talk impossible. The raw and hazardous weather suppressed any hope she had of leaving before morning.

Jared guided her down the steps, across the snow-covered lawn and around the corner of the garage to a well-stocked woodpile. Her foot slipped on a patch of ice, and she would have tumbled had he not yanked her back, slamming her against him to break her fall. Through the down of his jacket, she detected the iron strength of rock-hard muscles. Whatever Jared had been doing the last two years, he hadn't sat around going soft. He had the muscles and reflexes of a trained athlete, and a strength that could snap her in two.

"You okay?" His breath warmed her ear.

She nodded and struggled to regain her footing. Keeping her arm locked tightly in his, he steered her to the edge of the woodpile, where he stacked logs into her outstretched arms. In spite of the cold, heat prickled her nape. Surely it was her imagination, but she felt as if she was being watched. Jared might not believe her, but she was sure she'd seen something out here . . . Someone.

"Too heavy?" Jared called against the wind.

The look in his eyes dared her to say yes. Maybe he was testing her resolve.

"No!" she yelled against the wind's roar, staggering under the weight. "Give me a few more."

A flash of admiration lit his face before he stooped, picked up some sticks of kindling and added them to her burden. Tucking his own load of logs beneath one arm, he led her back inside.

The chilly house seemed warm after the freezing blasts of ice and snow. Tyler unloaded her burden into the woodbox by the fireplace, removed her sodden jacket, and waited for Jared to build up the fire. As soon as he'd settled into his deep leather chair, her eyes flitted anxiously toward the window. Perhaps she'd seen an animal. To get her mind off the figure in the snow, she confronted Jared.

"Now, don't you have a long story you were going to tell me?" The first rule of survival was Know Thine Enemy. She smiled into his scowling face. "I love long stories before the fire."

Jared grimaced at her. "You never give up, do you?"

"One of my better qualities. Makes me a helluva researcher."

"Or a colossal pain in the—neck, depending on your point of view."

Still frowning, Jared pulled himself out of his chair and headed for the kitchen, returning with a bottle of brandy and two snifters. He poured the amber liquid into one of the glasses and offered it to her, but she shook her head. After the dinner wine, brandy would put her to sleep, and she had no intention of dozing off before she heard what Jared had to say. Then she would lock herself in her room for the night.

As if fortifying himself for an ordeal, he swigged down the contents of the glass, then leaned back in his chair and closed his eyes. Firelight played across the strong planes of his face, bathing them in a glow that, combined with his unusual stillness, made him appear like the golden statue of some ancient mythic god. Only an occasional tremor of pain rippling across his features indicated that he was still awake.

She sat motionless, waiting. If she spoke again, she might destroy the effort he was building to divulge his story. The fire burned low, and she quietly added more logs against the encroaching cold.

When Jared finally spoke, his voice startled her, ringing strongly in the unnatural quiet of the spacious room. "Two years ago, I was working on a story about gunshot victims in D.C. I'd questioned the heads of trauma units in all the major hospitals in the area but one, and I was anxious to complete that interview so I could finish the story."

He glanced at Tyler, whose wide eyes locked on him like a laser, and he guessed she would know if he lied. He wouldn't change the truth, but he didn't have to tell her everything. No one except him knew everything. Not even his doctors.

"I was waiting in the emergency room to interview Dr. Gilleland after he came off duty. I have vivid memories of a man waiting across from me. His face had been slashed open from temple to chin, and he sat there, holding a towel to stanch the bleeding and staring at me with vacant eyes. Then my head exploded with pain. I must have lost all consciousness, because that man is the last thing I remember before waking up days later in the intensive-care unit."

A tremor shook his body. Talking about it was harder than he'd thought. He poured more brandy and bolted it down. The heat of the liquor seared his throat. "An aneurysm had burst in my brain."

Tyler gasped. "If you hadn't been at the emergency room—"

"I'd never have made it. Things were touch and go, as it was."

He shifted in his chair, avoiding her probing gaze. There had been many times since, when he'd wondered if he would be better off dead, rather than living with the hell that had followed his illness. "I don't remember how long I was hospitalized, but when they finally released me, I came here to recuperate. Been here ever since."

"Did you ever write your story on gunshot victims?"

He nodded. "Finished it while I was on sick leave. As soon as I'd sent it to the paper, I resigned."

"You had a job most journalists would die for. Why resign?"

Because he'd become a freak, a man unlike all others. How could he function in a world that reminded him every day of his own peculiarity? "Grandfather Slater died before my rebellion against the tobacco industry and left me a generous trust fund. I'd always wanted to write what I pleased, so I grabbed the opportunity."

"If you had the trust fund all along, why work for the *Post* at all?"

"Experience."

That wasn't a total lie, but he'd planned on years more experience before retiring to the mountains to write the "great American novel." He studied Tyler regretfully. The woman didn't miss a trick. He needed the assistance of a mind like that, but he had no choice but to send her away to safety—and soon.

Tyler watched his eyelids flutter and close and heard his heavy, even breathing. He'd fallen asleep, sprawled in his chair. She tiptoed to her room, removed a blanket from one of the twin beds, then carried it to the great room where she covered him against the cold.

Thick lashes lay against his cheeks, and sleep softened the rugged contours of his face, making him appear vulnerable—an enticing illusion, since Jared Slater had the strength of three men. She'd sensed his power when he saved her from crashing to the ice outside. A powerful man with secrets.

She retreated to her corner of the sofa with a snifter of brandy. She could sleep now. Jared had done his talking for the night, but he hadn't told her the whole story. Something terrible lurked in the depths of his eyes. Some pain too deep for words generated the wounded look that frightened her and, at the same time, made her long to gather him in her arms and comfort him.

She should lock herself in the bedroom to sleep, especially since she still had the strange sensation of being watched, but drowsiness overcame her. She tugged the afghan around her and nodded off.

THE BITING COLD awakened Tyler, and when she opened her eyes, gray dawn illuminated the tall east windows. Jared still slept in the chair across from her, but the fire was almost out, and the room's temperature had dropped. Careful not to awaken him, she shredded newspapers, laid kindling and logs, and soon had the blaze roaring again in the massive stone fireplace.

In the morning light, she laughed at her nervousness and fantasies of the night before. Jared Slater hadn't murdered her in her sleep—he hadn't even snored. The figure she'd seen outside was surely what Jared had said it was—nothing more than shadows. She didn't think the weather had improved enough for her to travel. Maybe, she thought, glancing at Jared, she no longer wanted to.

She performed her morning ritual in the bathroom, yearning for a hot shower, but making do with icy water splashed on her face and hands. She had just rinsed her mouth after brushing her teeth when Jared's agonized cry pierced the morning silence, making her blood run cold.

She rushed down the hall to the great room. He sat upright with a wild look in his eyes, and, in spite of the room's chill, sweat beaded his broad forehead.

"Jared?"

Ignoring her, he bolted from his chair, folded back the doors beneath the loft, and rummaged in his desk, grabbing a pencil and legal pad. Without acknowledging her presence, he returned to his chair and began to write furiously.

"What is it?" His frenzied behavior revived her suspicions.

"Don't interrupt," he said with a snarl, still writing.

She settled on the sofa and watched as he scribbled quickly, paused, closed his eyes as if remembering, then wrote again. When he'd finished, he read over the papers, groaned, and fell back in his chair.

"Are you all right?" she asked.

He breathed heavily, like a long-distance runner hitting the tape at the finish line. When he lifted his head and stared at her, his eyes were glazed. "Yeah, I'm fine."

"You look awful."

He rubbed his eyes, then combed both hands through his unruly hair. "Flattery doesn't work on me, if you're still trying for the job."

She ignored his taunt. "Maybe you'll feel better after a wash and some breakfast."

She eyed the legal pad beside him. Its filled pages resembled those on the nightstand in the bedroom. Maybe Jared was one of those writers who mulled over his material in his sleep and committed it to paper upon rising. But that didn't explain why he had cried out in pain, like an animal pinned in a steel trap.

"You're right. I need to flush the cobwebs out of my brain." He rose with a groan, picked up the pad, and took the stairs three at a time to the loft bathroom.

Only one thing was certain about Jared Slater—he was a puzzle. She gathered last night's glasses from the coffee table and was carrying them to the kitchen when a familiar sound stopped her. He was taking a shower. The thought of bathing in cold water in the icy room brought goose bumps to her skin, and she shivered violently.

In her room, she stripped and dressed in clean clothes, hoping that jeans, a flannel shirt, and her UNC sweatshirt in Carolina blue would provide more warmth than the clothes she'd just removed.

When she returned to the great room, Jared was lighting a Coleman stove he'd set on the granite kitchen counter. He grinned when he saw her, showing no trace of the tortured writer she'd witnessed earlier. "I raided the camping equipment in the utility room. Hot breakfast coming up."

"You're a miracle worker. I could die for a cup of coffee right now."

His grin faded. "Dying isn't required, but you will have to wait for the water to boil."

His hair, still wet from his shower, glistened in the morning sun, and he appeared warm and comfortable in snug jeans that hugged his narrow hips. He'd pulled a midnight-blue ski sweater over a white turtleneck.

He rummaged through the cabinets, and as the water in the saucepan began to boil, added oatmeal, raisins, chopped dried apples, cinnamon, brown sugar, and walnuts. The spice from his concoction permeated the kitchen with a homey, comforting aroma, making her hungry.

They ate without speaking, Jared preoccupied and Tyler hoping her quietness would encourage him to talk. A vertical line creased his forehead between his brows. She didn't have to be a trained psychologist to know that whatever he'd written on his legal pad earlier still disturbed him and that he was reluctant to talk about it.

After they'd cleared the dishes and settled before the fire, Tyler asked, "What were you writing this morning?"

He sat, neither moving nor speaking, staring at the flames as if he hadn't heard. His unnatural stillness ate at her nerves.

"Look," she said, "if telling me what was going on makes you uncomfortable, forget it. Let's talk about something else."

He stood, grasped the mantel with outstretched arms, propped one foot on the raised hearth, and stared at the flames. His body pulsed with latent power—and sorrow. What did he know that was so horrible, unspeakable?

She remembered news stories of a serial killer who had hidden the bodies of his victims in the woods surrounding his mountain retreat in Alabama, but she forced the memory away. Jared Slater was no murderer. She would stake her life on it.

She already had.

He turned and braced an elbow on the mantelpiece. "Why do you think I advertised for a research assistant?"

She shrugged. "To help gather information for your writing?"

He shook his head. "I'm a trained journalist. Whatever information I need for my stories, I can dig up for myself."

"Unless it's easier to let someone else do the drudge work and pay for it from Grandfather Slater's trust fund." Her anger over his reluctance to employ her simmered just below the boiling point, and sarcasm tinged her voice.

Before he could reply, the telephone rang in the loft bedroom, and he bounded up the stairs. The low murmur of his voice carried over the loft wall, but she couldn't make out his words.

Then realization hit her. The telephone lines were still working. She scurried across the room and unzipped her computer from its carrying case.

Jared met her at the foot of the stairs. "That was Farmer Sweeney at the foot of the mountain, calling to see if I was okay."

"Are you?" Tyler scanned his face. The terrible pain that had lurked in his eyes earlier had disappeared, leaving behind warm pools of soft brown that sent a shudder of pleasure up her spine.

"What's that?" He nodded toward her hands.

"My laptop computer."

"Battery pack?" Excitement colored his words.

"You got it. With the phone lines intact, we can hook up the modem, and we're in business—until the battery dies." Satisfaction surged within her. He'd said he was on deadline. If she could convince him to let her begin work, maybe he would change his mind about hiring her.

His mind raced as he connected Tyler's modem to the phone line. The information he'd received that morning tightened the crunch on his time. If he couldn't gather the data he needed—and soon—another woman might die. He walled off memories of his nightmare of Tyler, lying dead before his fireplace. He needed an assistant now more than ever. He would have to risk it—risk her—at least for a little while.

He chose his words so carefully that he might have been stepping through a minefield. "I've been giving the research-assistant position some thought."

Her head snapped up and gray eyes bore into him. "And?"

That slight movement of her head sent the perfumed aroma of her hair drifting beneath his nostrils, and desire gripped him. He resisted the impulse to push a stray curl off the pink curve of her cheek and struggled for control. He would never get the job done if he allowed her to distract him.

"I'd like you to begin work—on a temporary basis."

She jerked her thumb toward her computer. "Desperate times require desperate measures, huh?"

He couldn't restrain his smile. "Something like that."

She eyed him warily. "I don't get it. You knew last night the power would be out, but that didn't incline you toward hiring me then. Do you want me for my-self or my hard drive?''

His grin widened. God, he loved a woman with spunk. "Let's just say I could never resist a woman with such incredible assets."

She laughed. "I like you when you smile, Jared Slater. When's the last time you laughed?"

He reflected over the past two dismal years. "I can't remember."

She reached forward tentatively and touched the dimple at the corner of his mouth. "That's what I thought."

He grabbed her hand to thrust it away, but the warmth in her eyes made him pause, savoring the heat of her fingers and the throb of her pulse. "You haven't answered me about taking the job on a temporary ba-sis."

Her soft lips parted slightly over even, white teeth, and her breath formed a delicate cloud in the room's frigid air. "I wouldn't think you'd have to ask. You know how much I want this position."

What was happening to her? Mesmerized by his eyes, she checked the urge to draw closer, to warm herself against the broad hardness of his chest. She'd come to the mountains for work, not romance.

Wriggling beneath his gaze, she stared out the tall windows to where snow covered the trees. The sun shone fiercely in a sky of brilliant blue, highlighting the surrounding mountain peaks in crisp detail and reflecting off the waters of Lake Toxaway, which was sparkling in the deep cleft of the valley like a sapphire set in cotton batting. Just past the edge of the drive, a patch of darkness flashed through the trees.

"Look." She pointed out the window.

"What is it?"

"I thought I saw someone again." She crossed to the window, shaded her eyes against the glare and peered down the mountainside.

He followed her gaze but could detect no sign of movement on the sloping drive. "Maybe it was a trick of light again—or a small animal."

"It was bigger than that," she insisted.

He shrugged. "Maybe it was a bear or deer. There're a lot of both in the area. Are you ready to work?"

She sat at the desk and flipped up the screen on her laptop. "What's first?"

"I need to know every state where Spanish moss grows."

She swiveled in her chair and regarded him with a look of disbelief. "You're on a deadline for *this?*"

He glared at her. "Do you want the job or not?"

"Right, states with Spanish moss, coming up." Her fingers flew over the keyboard as she punched in codes and Internet addresses.

Jared watched her, bending over the keyboard toward the screen, taking notes from the information that scrolled there. She was just what he needed. He'd known it the moment he'd read her résumé, and she'd confirmed it with her spirited insistence on being hired.

He sighed with regret. She believed she'd won him over, but he would send her on her way later today, as soon as the snow began to melt, and long before the rhododendron bloomed.

THE SUN WAS SLIDING toward the western peaks when she handed him a sheaf of papers.

"The list of states is fairly short," she said, "but the list of cities with intersections of Orange and First is formidable."

"Thanks." He tucked the papers into his desk drawer and steeled himself for the unpleasant task ahead.

"What now?" she asked.

He extracted his checkbook from a cubbyhole and filled in a check. "Now we say goodbye."

Her head snapped up and her eyes narrowed. She nodded toward the drawer where he'd stashed the papers. "You didn't even look at my work. I assure you it's what you asked for."

"I have no doubt of it." He handed her the check. "But you've been so busy, perhaps you've failed to notice that the temperature's risen and the snow is melting. You won't have any problems getting off the mountain now."

"But what about my job?"

"The job isn't yours—it never has been."

"I'll sue—"

"Do whatever you must, but I can't endanger you by allowing you to stay here." He scowled at her, ignoring his desire to sweep her into his arms and kiss the determined set of her lips until they relaxed, turning warm and pliant beneath his own.

Without another word, she zipped her computer into its case and pulled on her coat. Her high cheekbones flushed bright red.

"I'll bring your bags," he said.

"How thoughtful." Her sarcasm stung his conscience, and without a backward glance, she walked to the front door and flung it open.

As she stepped across the threshold, she turned toward him again. "Goodbye, Jared Slater. Thanks for—"

A shot rang out from the woods beyond the clearing, and pain blossomed in her head.

Chapter Three

The blast from his .357 Magnum knocked the young woman off her feet and into the house beyond his view. No matter. He'd aimed for her head, a fatal shot.

In his stubbornness last night, he'd almost ruined everything, falling asleep in the cold. And when he'd awakened, the woman had spotted him and alerted Slater. But he had patience on his side. Stalking and killing consumed him, and inevitable death was all that mattered. *When* the dying occurred was an insignificant detail.

Last night he'd retreated to his Blazer at the foot of Slater's drive, where he had taken shelter against the wind and cold and grabbed a little shut-eye. All day today, after the long, uncomfortable night, the young woman had stayed out of sight.

Now, he sprinted down the gravel road toward his car, avoiding patches of ice not yet melted by the sun. His breath came in tortured gasps. He wasn't as young or as fit as he'd once been, but that was no matter, either. He wasn't a lot of things now—except a patient, skillful killer.

He scrambled into his Blazer and gunned the engine. The law would arrive soon—and the coroner. And he would lie low until time for the next one to die.

THE BOOMING GUNFIRE reverberated in Tyler's ears, and pain swelled in her head. She felt herself lifted off her feet and slammed onto the floor as a terrible weight bore down on her. Dazed, she took a few seconds to realize the heaviness that crushed her was Jared Slater.

She'd heard only one shot. Maybe it had struck him. As far as she knew, she was fine. Or maybe she was in shock. She twisted beneath him.

"Lie still," he ordered in a whisper.

At least he was alive. "Are you hit?"

"Be quiet," came the fierce reply. "And stay put."

His weight lifted, and he wriggled toward the entrance like an army commando. Remaining on his stomach, he slammed the door shut, reached up and secured the lock. He crawled at an amazing pace, levering himself on knees and elbows behind the sofa and up the stairs.

She bit her lip to keep from crying out. Through the uncovered windows, the stairway to the loft was clearly visible to anyone outside. She held her breath, waiting for the sound of another shot, then gasped with relief as Jared disappeared into the loft bedroom.

The low murmur of his voice drifted down from above, too softly for her to discern his words. A minute later, he appeared again on the stairs, clearing them with a leap and diving toward her.

He tapped her shoulder. "Follow me."

Scurrying again on all fours, he rounded the counter that separated the great room from the kitchen. Expecting to be shot any second, she hastened after him on her hands and knees into the shelter of the kitchen, out of sight of the immense wall of windows that made them a sitting target for anyone watching from outdoors.

Breathless, she pulled herself into a sitting position and leaned against a counter. "What the hell is going on?"

Jared shushed her and closed his eyes, every muscle of his body tense and alert, waiting. She strained to hear what he was listening for, but blood thundered in her ears, drowning out all sounds except the rasp of his ragged breathing and her own.

This couldn't be happening to her. Librarians were supposed to live quiet, ordered lives with their tranquillity broken only by the occasional overdue book. When she'd signed on as a research assistant, dodging bullets was the last thing she'd expected.

"My God, you're hit!" His voice exploded like a shot in the stillness.

She glanced down at her bloodstained sweatshirt, lifted her hand to her throbbing temple, and gingerly extracted a long sliver from beneath her skin. Uncomprehending, she stared at it. "It's wood, not a bullet."

He cupped her face in his hand as he examined the wound. "There's a lot of blood on your shirt, but the wound looks superficial. I'll drive you to the clinic after the sheriff leaves."

"What sheriff?"

He removed his hand, and she suppressed the desire to clutch it against her cheek again, to recapture the assurance of his warmth and strength.

He resumed his vigil. "I called him when I went for my gun."

Only then did she notice the butt of an automatic pistol protruding from his belt. "Somebody out there almost killed me, and you're sitting here, armed to the teeth. I think I deserve an explanation."

Tiny creases formed around his eyes. "If I had one, you'd be welcome to it. I'm hoping the sheriff can tell us what's going on."

He leaned against the cabinet with an expression that squelched further questions.

Time stretched and slowed as they waited for the sheriff, and a damp chill burgeoned in the room as the fire dwindled and went out. When she shivered in the nippy air, he drew her close, cradling her against his side, warming her with the heat of his lean, muscled body, enveloping her in a one-armed embrace that kept his other hand free for the gun at his belt.

The protracted time sharpened her senses, increasing her awareness of his body. Its heat radiated a pleasant aroma of soap and woodsmoke, mixed with his uniquely masculine scent. His heartbeat thudded against her cheek, which was pressed against his chest, and, in spite of the lurking danger outside, she relaxed in his embrace.

After what seemed hours, the crunch of tires on gravel announced the arrival of a vehicle, but when she attempted to stand, Jared pulled her back roughly and pressed a warning finger to his lips. Until then, she hadn't considered that the car might belong to the same person who had fired at her, and the thought sent her skittering pulse into overdrive.

She jumped in alarm when someone banged on the front door. Jared's arm tightened around her.

A booming voice vibrated through the door. "Slater, it's Sheriff Tillett. You okay in there?"

Jared climbed to his feet and held out a hand to her. Cramped muscles screamed in protest as she rose and followed him. When he unlocked the door and swung it wide, the shattered doorframe, just inches from where her head had been when the shot sounded, drew her attention. If the bullet had hit her instead . . .

"Ma'am, do you need a doctor?" Sheriff Tillett's voice cut through her giddiness. "Should I call an ambulance?"

She drew a deep breath to drive away her nausea. "I'll be fine. I was hit by a flying splinter, that's all."

Jared stepped back from the door. "We'll be safer inside until we know who's out there."

Tillett, whose beefy frame filled the doorway, removed his broad-brimmed hat and stepped into the room. "Two of my deputies are scouring the mountain, but it's pretty deserted this time of year."

She lit candles on the mantelpiece, and Jared drew the curtains, blocking the view of the room from anyone still lingering in the surrounding woods.

Tillett eased his uniformed bulk into a chair. Weathered skin sagged over his square face, and his eyes held the weary look of a man who didn't get enough rest. "Did you see who fired at you?"

She shook her head. "There's been no sign of anyone—"

The sheriff lifted bushy eyebrows at her pause.

She shrugged. The shadowy figure at the window last night seemed even less real in the light of day. It had to have been a bear or deer or just shadows. She couldn't be certain she'd seen anyone that afternoon. "Not really."

The officer turned his attention to Jared. "Know anybody who'd want to harm you or yours?"

Jared pushed his thick hair off his forehead. The haunted gleam returned to his eyes, and his face appeared gaunt in the candlelight. "I've been here almost two years now, Sheriff, and I keep to myself. I haven't had the opportunity to make any enemies."

Tillett scratched his chin thoughtfully and lifted his bushy eyebrows in a grin. "Betcha made plenty people mad when you wrote for that big D.C. paper."

When Jared smiled, her nervousness deserted her, replaced by a tingling sensation that chased the chill from her bones.

"Too many to count," Jared agreed, "but if they were angry enough to kill, they'd have come after me long before now."

Tillett nodded. "What about you, Mrs. Slater?"

She blushed at his assumption. "I'm Tyler Harris, Mr. Slater's research assistant."

"Sorry, ma'am." He drilled her with intense blue eyes, making her thankful for a clear conscience. "Any reason someone might want to harm you?"

She laughed at the absurdity of his question. "I only arrived from Chapel Hill last night. No one but my grandmother even knows I'm here."

Jared turned from the fireplace where he'd rekindled the blaze. "Why this line of questioning, Sheriff? Maybe the shot was fired by a sportsman, hunting out of season."

Tillett dug into the pocket of his leather jacket and held out a small object in the palm of his hand. "Hunting with a handgun? Before I knocked, I pried this slug out of your doorframe. Looks like either a .38 or a .357—not your average hunter's weapon of choice."

Jared shrugged. "Then maybe it was kids, plinking at targets in the woods. Those bullets travel a long distance."

"Maybe," Tillett said in a noncommittal tone. He indicated her bags, scattered by the door. "The two of you should stay inside until we complete our sweep of the area, just to be safe.''

Jared closed the door behind Tillett and secured the dead bolt. Darkness had fallen quickly in the mountains, and gloom obscured the corners of the room, but the candles provided enough illumination to distinguish Tyler's head wound, the bloodstains on her clothes, and the shell-shocked glaze in her eyes.

''I should clean that wound,'' he said.

She started at the sound of his voice and glanced down at her clothes. With a swift, impatient movement, she tugged the soiled sweatshirt over her head, her firm breasts straining against the plaid fabric of her shirt.

Desire washed through him as he recalled the sensation of her body against his as they'd huddled in the kitchen, waiting for the sheriff. When the gunshot had sounded and he'd yanked her from the doorway and covered her body to protect her, he'd feared his prophetic dream had come true, especially once he'd witnessed the gash at her temple and blood on her shirt.

But her wound was superficial, and she stood in front of him now, shaken but whole. Hope soared within him. Maybe the consequences in his dreams weren't inevitable, after all. Better yet, maybe the curse that had befallen him two years ago had lifted. If he could prevent the murder of the woman in the town where Spanish moss grew, he would know for sure.

He gathered swabs, antiseptic and bandages from the bathroom and returned to the great room. Tyler huddled near the blaze on the raised hearth, where firelight sparkled on her hair, creating rivers of flame in the jet-black strands. Heat reddened her cheeks, and she studied the flickering logs with pensive eyes.

At the sight of her, protectiveness mingled with his desire. He would test his theory, but he refused to put her at any more risk. In his dream, her death had occurred with the rhododendron in full bloom. The unseasonable cold would delay its flowering, so she would be safe with him for a few days longer.

With her assistance, he might foil the upcoming murder and catch the killer.

And keep her with you a few days longer before you have to send her away for good, an inner voice taunted.

He closed his mind and shoved away the pain of isolation he'd suffered the past two years. He'd become a freak, an outcast, avoiding everyone except those who might help him track the killer who roamed his mind and the byways of the eastern United States. Tyler Harris had brought him respite from that loneliness and the pleasure of relating to someone else besides a murderer.

He sat beside her on the stone hearth, grasped her chin, and tipped her head to examine her wound more clearly. When he swabbed the broken skin with antiseptic, her swift intake of breath informed him that it stung.

"Sorry," he said. "I didn't mean to hurt you."

She hoped the glow from the fire hid the heat in her face. He hadn't hurt her at all. She'd reacted to the disturbing nearness of him and his very kissable lips hovering inches from hers as he cleaned the cut on her forehead.

She closed her eyes against temptation. "You didn't hurt me."

As she spoke, she realized that her fear of him had vanished. The stranger at the service station couldn't have known what he was talking about. The strong but gentle man who cleaned her wounded forehead so tenderly would never harm anyone. She trusted that fact as well as she knew her own name.

But just because Jared wouldn't harm her didn't mean she was safe. She touched her sore temple tentatively. "Is this what you meant?"

His eyes clouded in puzzlement.

She resisted the impulse to smooth away the creases between his eyebrows. "You warned that if I worked for you there'd be risks involved."

He moved away from her into the shadows. "What I'm working on *is* dangerous, but I doubt it's connected to the shot that almost hit you. That had to be a freak accident—target shooters, like I told the sheriff."

She peered into the gloom, attempting to see his face. "How can you be sure?"

At the window's edge, he lifted the drapery and peered out. Silence swelled in the room, broken only by the hiss and crackle of the fire. A minute later, he returned to one of the deep chairs in front of the hearth. "I'm not sure. It's been a long time since I've been certain about anything."

The agony in his voice wrenched her heart, and she resisted the urge to go to him, to embrace him and ease his pain. The ramrod straightness of his back, the determined jut of his chin, and the forthright expression on his handsome face rebuffed her. An inveterate loner, Jared wouldn't appreciate her consoling him.

He lay back against the headrest and clasped the chair arms until his knuckles whitened. If it hadn't been for the stiffness of his posture, she would have sworn he slept. Tension blended with the silence in the room. She longed to comfort him with words, but, ignorant of the source of his pain, she didn't know what to say.

Finally he spoke, his words shattering the tension in the room like a hammer splintering glass. "When I told you about my illness, I didn't tell you everything."

She squelched her raging curiosity and shrugged. "You don't owe me an explanation. You've made your position clear. I'll leave in the morning."

"I'd like you to stay a few more days—" he held up his hands, palms outward "—but don't answer yet. Hear me out first."

He lay back again and stared into the hidden recesses of the beamed ceiling. His eyes glittered like dark diamonds in the dim light, and emotions scudded across the stark angles of his face. "Two years ago, after I awoke from the operation that repaired the burst aneurysm in my brain, I discovered my vision had gone haywire. Fantastic auras surrounded every person who entered my room."

"Auras?"

"Halos of light. And all different colors, depending on the person who projected them. I questioned the neurologist about them, and he didn't seem concerned. Said they were possibly a by-product of the surgery and would probably disappear as I healed."

"Did they?" She'd read about such phenomena, usually associated with so-called psychics, but she didn't believe in sixth sense. In her book, if she couldn't see, taste, touch, smell, or hear something, it didn't exist.

He straightened and leaned toward her with his hands clasped between his knees. "They disappeared, all right. I wish to God they hadn't."

"Why?"

"Because that's when the dreams started."

She wanted to assure him that everyone dreamed, but seeing the tortured expression on his face, she bit back her reply. "What kind of dreams?"

"Nightmares."

She rose from the hearth and settled, cross-legged, on the floor at his feet. "We've all had nightmares."

He reached out and traced the bandage on her temple with a gentle finger. "Not like these."

"If talking about them upsets you, let's change the subject." She pulled his hand from her forehead and held it, twining his cool fingers with her own, relishing the touch of his flesh against hers.

With his free hand, he smoothed her hair, scorching her with a look that sent her pulse thundering. "You have to know about the dreams before you can decide whether to stay."

She scooted across the floor and leaned back against the seat of his chair. Maybe the telling would be easier if he didn't have to face her. "I'm listening."

"I chalked up the first dream as an ordinary nightmare—" his voice echoed in the dark room "—a vestige from my days covering the crime beat. But the dream kept recurring in the same unaltering detail."

He stroked her hair again, as if gaining assurance from the contact. "In my dream, the same woman died, over and over, and I was the one who stalked her, who fired the fatal shot, who stood over the body until I was certain she was dead."

He fell silent, and the quiet grew uncomfortable.

"Maybe your dream was symbolic," she said, "and the woman represented something in your life you wanted ended."

"You should have been a psychiatrist." She could hear the smile in his voice. "That's what the shrink they referred me to suggested. And he almost had me convinced, until I was well enough to request back issues of the *Post* to check out a series I'd written just before my illness."

He stood and stretched, then crossed to the windows and peeked outside. When he turned, he remained hidden in the shadows and his disembodied voice floated across the room. ''In the edition printed the day after my surgery, a woman's picture appeared—Veronica Molinsky, the same woman I'd seen in my dream.''

He stepped from the gloom into the candlelight. ''She'd been shot to death.''

Remembering the stranger's warning, she felt a tingle of fear skitter down her spine before her common sense took hold again. ''Maybe you saw her picture at the newspaper office on the desk of the reporter writing the story.''

''Before the fact? The coroner placed the time of death around ten o'clock, precisely the time I arrived at the trauma unit for my interview with Dr. Gilleland.'' Torment etched the planes of his handsome face.

Her instincts had been right. ''Then you couldn't be the killer.''

''Me, the killer?'' He shook his head. ''But I *know* the killer.''

''Have you told the police?''

''It's not that simple.'' He collapsed in his chair and raked his fingers through his hair. ''You see, I know the killer's mind, but I don't know his name or his face.''

She swallowed hard. He'd just entered the *Twilight Zone*. Maybe the aneurysm in his brain had been repaired, but it had obviously left him damaged, delusional. "How can you know the killer's mind if you don't know who he is?"

He stared at her with eyes void of light. "Because he haunts my dreams. Veronica Molinsky was only the first victim."

"There've been more?" The poor guy had really gone off the deep end.

She jumped as a sharp rapping reverberated through the room and Sheriff Tillett's voice filtered through the front door. She'd been so entranced by Jared's story, she hadn't heard the sheriff's vehicle approach.

"I won't come in," he said when Jared opened the door. "Just wanted to report my men and I have searched the mountain, and it's deserted, except for Sweeney at his farm. Tourists won't arrive for another month."

Jared appeared calm and rational, not the tortured man of a few moments earlier, Tyler thought.

"No sign of our shooter?" he asked.

"Just some tire tracks," the sheriff returned. "In the mud at the foot of your drive. Might have been somebody from town trying out a new gun, thinking nobody lived here this time of year. Whoever it was is long gone."

"Thanks for checking. Sorry to have troubled you," Jared said.

"No trouble." The sheriff replaced his hat and tapped the broad brim in a salute. "Just doing my job.

By the way, power crews are on the mountain, so your electricity should be restored soon.''

Jared locked the door and turned to her. ''Looks like the coast is clear, for now.''

The sheriff's explanation bothered her. ''Odd that someone would try a new gun and only shoot it once.''

He lifted an eyebrow. ''Whoever fired the shot could have realized he'd hit something and taken off to avoid the consequences.''

''Maybe.''

Tyler studied her mysterious host. Jared's rational demeanor and words contradicted his wild story moments earlier of a killer haunting his dreams. Her thoughts whirled in confusion. One minute, all she wanted was to pick up her bags and rush out the door, off the mountaintop, and back to the security of home. The next minute, the thought of never seeing Jared Slater again filled her with sorrow. The man was a whole catalog of contradictions—infuriating and yet sensitive, arrogant and yet humble, mesmerizing and yet frightening. In a word, he was fascinating. He drew her to him the way a compass was drawn to the North Star.

She would never make a prudent choice in his disturbing company. She glanced toward her bags and computer, which had remained by the front door. If she left now, she could stay overnight at the motel in Brevard and decide in the morning whether to drive home or return to the mountain.

He followed her gaze. ''Don't go yet, please.''

Lights blinked on in the kitchen and the refrigerator hummed, announcing that electrical service had resumed.

"At least have supper with me. Then I'll tell you the rest of my story."

If she hadn't looked at him, she could have picked up her bags and left, but his lopsided smile, underlaid with a sense of terrible isolation, melted her resolve.

While Jared prepared supper, and later, as they devoured bowls of thick vegetable soup and grilled cheese sandwiches, she hoped he'd forgotten his strange tale. They talked of the Tar Heels' winning basketball season, a particular politician's latest tirade in the Senate, and compared favorite hiking trails along the Blue Ridge Parkway. As they talked, Tyler avoided mention of his tale about the nightmares.

When they'd finished after-dinner coffee in front of the fire, she set her cup aside and stood. The mantel clock read eight-fifteen—still early enough for her to drive to Brevard and find a room for the night.

He followed her to the door. "What about the job?"

She met his eyes—a definite mistake—then tore her gaze away. "I'll call you from the motel in the morning and let you know. Good night, Jared."

THE STRANGER TOSSED on the uncomfortable mattress in his Brevard motel room, threw back the covers, and stumbled across the floor to the bathroom.

With trembling fingers, he uncapped an aspirin bottle, then washed the tablets down with a cola gone flat.

Damn his stupid impatience. If he hadn't spent the night on the mountain, he wouldn't have caught a cold. And if he hadn't been shaken with chills, he wouldn't have missed his shot. He'd waited in his car behind the summer cottage at the foot of the mountain until the sheriff and his deputies had passed, but there had been no sign of the coroner's wagon. That meant the woman was still alive.

No matter. His cold wouldn't last forever, and the next time he saw her, he wouldn't miss.

Unable to sleep with his sinuses congested, he turned off the lights in his room, opened the draperies, and with his revolver on his lap, sat watching the parking lot. He didn't think the lawmen had seen him, but he would stay alert and watch the parking lot, just to make sure.

Chapter Four

Jared ignored Tyler's farewell and stood between her and the door while he warred with his own conscience. Sending her away might keep her safe, but without her help, the next victim was doomed. With a twinge of guilt, he conceded his desire to keep her with him for as long as possible.

For the first time in two years, his isolation had been breached, the pain of his loneliness eased. In a few short hours, Tyler Harris had brought light and laughter into his life again with her witty conversation and spunky courage. And he would have to be a dead man to resist the charm of her appealing face and delectable curves. He'd known many women, but none had ever affected him as Tyler had. If she walked out the door now, he would be more alone than ever.

He placed his hands on her shoulders, but resisted the urge to draw her into his arms. "You can't make a decision about the job if you don't know all the facts."

Her eyes glinted like burnished silver in the firelight, and her fragrance tortured him with its sweetness. "I know enough."

"You know enough to think I'm crazy or dangerous or both." He slid his hands down her arms, took her bags and placed them by the door. "Give me forty-five minutes. Then, if you still want to leave, I'll call the motel in Brevard and make you a reservation."

"But it's getting late—"

In spite of her protests, she allowed him to lead her back to the chair before the fire.

At his small victory, a thrill of pleasure surged through him, followed quickly by dread. When she'd heard what he had to say, she might be more determined than ever to leave.

To delay exposing the demons of his dreams, he refilled her coffee cup and replenished the fire before settling in the chair opposite her.

Without an excuse to stall any longer, he plunged back into his story with all the enthusiasm of a man entering a burning building. "Veronica Molinsky was the first victim in my dreams, but she wasn't the last."

Tyler eyed him over the rim of her cup with an expression that revealed none of her thoughts. "How many others are there?"

"Two," he lied. He wouldn't frighten her with his vision of her death. When the time came to send her away for her own safety, she would be better off not knowing.

"Are they both dead?" Interest kindled in her eyes, and a hint of something else that pierced him like a spike—pity.

He leaned back in the chair and closed his eyes against her sympathy. "I'd better back up. None of this makes much sense, but it makes even less sense out of order.

"Once I had read the police reports and realized Veronica Molinsky died exactly as I'd dreamed, all I wanted was to escape. I was still too weak to work. Even the kind attentions of family and friends exhausted me. So I bought this house and moved here, hoping tranquillity and mountain air would flush the nightmares from my brain."

He shut his eyes and when he grew quiet, she thought he'd fallen asleep. Poor guy. Evidently isolation had only worsened his delusions. Common sense urged her to race to her car and flee the mountaintop, but Jared Slater, a mesmerizing paradox, a man of steel and sinew who could best any opponent—except those without substance: his traumatic dreams—held her heart captive.

He opened his eyes again, staring through the dim light. "The dreams did stop for a while, and I attributed that to the fact I'd regained my strength."

He'd regained his strength, all right, as well as that of two others. "The mountain air?" she asked.

"Partly," he replied with a grin. "At first, all I could manage was the trek down the drive to the mailbox and back. After I'd begun working out with weights, I indulged myself in a new hobby, rock climbing.''

''I thought you didn't leave the mountain.''

''Didn't have to. Right behind the house is a sixty-foot rock face. I rappel down and claw my way back to the top. Does wonders for the muscles—and helps me sleep.''

She flinched in surprise when the clock on the mantel chimed the half hour. ''And you haven't dreamed of Veronica Molinsky again?''

He shook his head and a shock of fine brown hair tumbled across his high forehead. ''For the first six months, my dreams were nothing out of the ordinary. Then I began to have persistent dreams of a pleasant woman with dark hair laced with gray. She reminded me of my mother.''

She confronted him with raised brows. ''Your mother?''

The corners of his mouth twitched in a smile. ''Don't play armchair psychiatrist with me. I love my mother and have no unconscious desire to kill her.''

''Sorry.'' She blushed at having her thoughts read. ''What happened next?''

''At first the dreams were innocuous—simple scenes of the woman preparing meals, weeding her garden, playing with her grandchildren. The only odd thing about them was their repetitiveness.'' His grip tightened on the chair arm. ''But after a few weeks, they changed.''

When a burning log broke and crashed into the ashes of the fireplace, she jerked with alarm, revealing her tightly-strung nerves. "You dreamed then that she was murdered, too?"

"No." He massaged his temple as if his head ached, and she wondered if he still bore the scars of his operation beneath his hair. "It's difficult to explain. In my dreams, I was no longer me, but the killer who stalked her. I watched her through his eyes, felt his hatred and rage. I knew that she, too, just like Veronica Molinsky, was eventually going to die, killed by the same man."

Her heart hammered against her ribs. How could he know a killer's mind, unless the burst aneurysm had severed his sanity, creating a kind of Dr. Jekyll and Mr. Hyde—two personalities in one man, each unaware that the other existed. "Did you warn the woman?"

Anguish twisted the handsome lines of his face. "How could I? I had no idea who she was or what part of the country she lived in."

"So you did nothing?" She couldn't restrain the horror in her voice.

"I did everything I could." Slater rose and began to pace in front of the hearth. The fire cast his shadow across the room—a distorted version of him that loomed, frightening and overpowering, in the gloom. "I kept paper and pencil beside my bed and recorded every detail from the dreams."

She recalled the legal pad beside his bed and his cry of pain and frantic scribbling upon awakening that morning. "And you found her?"

He turned his back to the fire and thrust his hands into the back pockets of his jeans. "It took months. I finally narrowed down the section of the country to the Northeast by researching the trees, shrubs and flowers in her garden and the style and materials of her home."

She pictured him, fingers flying over his computer keyboard, racing against time. "Wasn't that like looking for a needle in a haystack?"

"First I had to find the haystack," he said with a wry grimace. "So I gleaned tidbits of information from my dreams. Her first name was Mary. Her husband's name was Pete. In one dream, I watched him empty the contents of his pockets onto his bureau. He carried a badge."

"A policeman?"

"A detective. I even saw his badge number."

His story became more unreal by the minute. "And you located him by his badge number?"

"If only it had been that easy. Do you know how many police departments there are in the Northeast?"

She shook her head. "How *did* you find the woman named Mary?"

"In one dream, I watched her drive by a college campus. I couldn't see its name, but a stone tablet on the entrance gate stated it had been founded in 1837.

By looking up all colleges established that year in the Northeast, I pinpointed a small town in Massachusetts.''

No wonder he needed a research assistant. Tracking down Mary's location must have taken weeks. "How long did it take to identify Mary after that?"

He slumped into his chair. "I boarded a plane that night to Boston and booked into a hotel at the airport.''

"Then you *did* leave the mountaintop." The fact disturbed her, shattering his alibi.

"I had no choice," he said in a toneless voice. "I had to warn Mary. That night at the airport, the killer closed in on her in my dream."

His distress throbbed like a palpable presence in the room. But Mary had been in real danger only once he found her, Tyler thought. She bit back her suspicions and waited for him to continue.

"As soon as I awoke, I rented a car and drove a hundred miles to the town where the college was located. I went straight to the police department, gave them the badge number, and asked to speak with Pete." He leaned forward and hid his face in his hands.

Compassion stabbed through her as she watched him relive the pain. Maybe all of it had happened only in his damaged mind. "You don't have to tell me all this."

"But I do. You have to know what to expect if you're going to work for me." A trace of a smile twitched the corners of his mouth. "Now you understand why the pay is so good."

His salary offer had been irresistible, but even more tantalizing was the man—an enigma she itched to unravel, if only to ease his grief. Whether he suffered from multiple personalities or psychotic delusions didn't matter. What mattered was that the man before her seemed honest, good, and decent, and didn't deserve what was happening to him.

"The man's name was Stanwick," Jared continued, "and the desk sergeant looked at me strangely when he gave me Pete's address. When I parked in front of Stanwick's house, I experienced a chilling sense of déjà vu. Everything was just as I'd dreamed it, right down to the pale blue flowers that bordered the front walk."

Jared levered himself out of his chair and crossed to the kitchen, removed the brandy bottle from its cupboard and poured himself a glass. "I'd offer you a drink, but you may be driving once my story's finished."

He gulped the brandy, and his face contorted as if he'd swallowed bitter medicine. "A young man, Mary's grown son, answered the door, and I asked to see Mary Stanwick. He led me into the living room, which seemed as familiar as my own house. The man I recognized as Pete was sitting on the sofa, staring at the floor."

Jared studied the bottle as if contemplating another drink. "I cleared my throat to announce my presence, and Pete lifted his head. I've never seen a man so devastated.''

"You were too late?" She yearned for a way to ease the pain that shone in Jared's eyes.

He succumbed to pouring another finger of brandy. "I feared I was, but I had to be sure. I asked again if I could speak with Mary."

He carried the brandy snifter back to his chair and sat, cradling it between his palms, pondering the amber liquid as if it held a secret he could unlock. "Stanwick looked like a man who had no tears left in him. He told me Mary had been shot to death in the church parking lot the previous night after leaving her quilting-club meeting."

Jared's agony tempered her skepticism. No one could really predict the future, but he *believed* he'd had foreknowledge of the danger to Mary Stanwick and had been unable to stop it.

She played along with his delusions. Maybe eventually they would make sense. "How did you explain your presence there?"

He gripped the glass so tightly she feared it would shatter in his hands. "I didn't. I just left."

"You left? That's it?" Irritation blended with sympathy. "What about the killer?"

He set the untouched drink aside. "I would have helped the police with their investigation if I could, but I knew nothing of any substance about the killer. If I'd gone to them with the story I told you, they would have locked me away as a signal-twenty."

"Signal-twenty?"

Another smile flitted briefly across the sturdy angles of his face. "That's police code for a crazy person. You've probably considered the possibility yourself."

Since she couldn't deny it, she ignored his question. "*If* I decide to stay, what would my duties be?"

He leaned forward, eyes blazing. Tortured he might be, but he didn't give in to despair. He emanated a sense of burning purpose and determination. "To help me catch this guy before he strikes again."

Jared appeared as sane as anyone, but she couldn't know for sure. She shook her head wearily, too tired to struggle with her emotions. "I'm a researcher. You'll have to find someone else to play Dr. Watson to your Sherlock."

He rose, grasped her hands and pulled her to her feet. "You've had a rough day. Why don't you get some sleep, and we'll talk about it in the morning."

Fatigue seeped through her. The alertness needed to navigate the twisting mountain roads had deserted her an hour ago. Staying the night might not be wise, but driving in her present state would be suicide.

"Okay." She stifled a yawn with the back of her hand. "But I'm not making any promises."

He brushed a curl off her cheek, and the warmth of his hand seared her skin. If the man was insane, she must be crazy, too, to be so drawn to him.

She followed him down the hallway as he carried her bags to the bedroom again. When she turned to bid him good-night, he grasped her shoulders and peered into her eyes.

"Thank you for listening." Her nerve endings resonated with his deep baritone. "You're the only one who's heard my story. I hope you'll decide to stay."

"Tomorrow," she muttered wearily. "We'll talk about it then."

She locked the door behind him and, as an extra precaution, jammed a chair beneath the knob. After dressing in warm pajamas, she crawled into bed and turned out the light. For a long time, sleep eluded her. She lay listening to branches scrape against her window and trying to convince herself she was safe because *she* wasn't the woman in Jared Slater's dreams.

THE CLICK OF THE doorknob awakened her. Disoriented in the pitch darkness, she couldn't remember where she was. She fumbled for the bedside lamp switch, and its soft light illuminated the travel clock she'd set out the night before. It was six o'clock in the morning. And she was in Jared Slater's guest room.

Still groggy from deep sleep, she watched the doorknob turn. Apprehension drove the dregs of stupor from her mind. She must have been insane to stay the night with Jared, a man with a killer in his head.

She cast about the room in search of an object, anything she could heft and use as a weapon. Her gaze fell on a walking stick--a solid club of heavy, twisted hickory that leaned in a corner. As she lunged across the room for it, a knock sounded at the door.

"Tyler, are you awake?" Jared's voice, strong and hearty, reverberated through the door panels.

He sounded sane enough. She relaxed her grip on the stick, inhaled deeply, and tried to reply in a normal tone. "It's 6:00 a.m. What do you want?"

"I brought your coffee. It's time to get to work."

She collapsed on the edge of the bed, wondering what to do. She had to open the door sometime, but she distrusted what she might find on the other side. Was it possible that the night had transformed Jared? Who would he be this morning—Dr. Jekyll or Mr. Hyde?

She couldn't remain huddled in the bedroom for the rest of her life, attempting to forestall the inevitable. With reluctance, she shuffled into her slippers and robe. Still clasping the walking stick, she slid the chair from beneath the knob and turned the key.

Jared heard the latch click. When the door swung inward, Tyler stared up at him, her face framed by thick, tangled hair, one hand clutching her robe beneath her chin. Uncertainty glistened in her eyes, still puffy from sleep. Her other hand held his carved hickory stick.

"A little early for a hike in the woods, isn't it?" He kept his voice light, hoping to put her at ease, and offered her a cup. "Here's your coffee. Breakfast will be ready in ten minutes."

Her eyes mirrored her indecision as she faced the choice of which hand should accept the mug he proffered. He breathed a sigh of relief when she leaned the walking stick against the doorjamb and accepted the steaming coffee with a mumbled thanks.

"There's plenty of hot water now," he said, "if you want a shower before breakfast."

With reluctance, Jared returned to the kitchen, carrying the image of her confusion and anxiety with him. If he'd been in her place, he would have never stayed this long. Between being shot at and listening to the ravings of a man who must seem a first-class lunatic, no wonder she seemed nervous.

He issued up a silent prayer that she would stay. He needed her to help him find the killer. Most of all, he needed her to make him feel human again, even if only for a few days until he had to send her away for her own safety.

The cozy warmth of the kitchen, the aroma of coffee, the muffled rumble of the shower, and the sizzle of sausage in the frying pan combined in a symphony of domestic harmony. Maybe somewhere in an alternate universe another Jared Slater existed in such peacefulness, about to enjoy a tranquil breakfast with a woman, unfettered by homicidal dreams and the compulsion to stop a madman before he killed again.

He shoved aside wistful thoughts. Sentimentality would only slow him down. Thirty minutes later, Tyler emerged in formfitting jeans and a red pullover with a crisp white collar protruding at the crew neckline. By then, he had tamped down his feelings so securely that his pulse barely accelerated at the sight of her. Her face was freshly-scrubbed and her eyes looked innocent. Her magnificent hair was fixed in a neat French braid. The tiny cut on her temple served as the only visible reminder of the trauma she'd endured the day before.

"Did you sleep well?" He set a plate laden with scrambled eggs, sausages and grits at her place opposite his on the counter.

She climbed onto the high stool. "Surprisingly. How about you—any more dreams?"

"Not last night, thank God. For once I actually feel rested, which is just as well. We have our work cut out for us today." He placed his own plate on the counter and took his seat. "That is, if you've decided to help."

With a sinking heart, he watched doubt flood her lovely features.

She sipped her orange juice slowly, as if deliberating what to say, and when she finally spoke, she chose her words with care, as if groping her way over unfamiliar terrain. "By your own admission, you suffered a severe injury to your brain a couple of years ago. How can you be sure these dreams aren't a result of that?"

"A figment of my imagination?" He struggled to keep the impatience from his voice. "That's a fair question. Maybe before you decide about working for me, you should check out the files on Veronica Molinsky and Mary Stanwick."

She nodded. "I will, but that doesn't mean—"

"Tyler—" he savored the sound of her name on his tongue "—I promise, you're safe with me."

He reached across the counter and grasped her hand, and contact with the seductive warmth of her skin crumbled the barrier he'd erected earlier around his emotions. He struggled to regain control. If he so much as hinted at the strength of his feelings, she would probably take off, spooked for good. "Don't let your breakfast get cold."

For distraction, he flicked on the television in the great room with the remote control, and they finished breakfast as they listened to the news from the Asheville station, including a forecast of warmer weather.

"I'll do the dishes," he said when they'd eaten, "while you check out my story."

He folded back the doors beneath the loft to uncover his desk and computer, then crossed to the windows and tugged open the draperies. Striations of pink, gold and mauve light tinged the eastern sky, bathing the pale gray bark of barren trees and the undergrowth of dogwood and wild azalea.

He heard the soft hiss of her breath beside him.

"It's beautiful," she said with a sigh.

The delicate light illuminated her face, and its glow seemed to emanate from within her, reminding him of a Botticelli angel.

"Beautiful," he agreed.

He rammed his hands into his pockets to keep from clutching her to him and returned to the kitchen. She started to work, while he did the dishes. Over the rattle of silverware in the sink, computer keys clicked softly in the morning stillness.

He'd put away the last pan, when he realized the sound had stopped. He turned to find Tyler standing at the counter, studying him with an expression he couldn't interpret.

"I've accessed back issues of the newspapers in D.C. and Mary Stanwick's town," she said. "Your story of the murders checks out."

He folded a dish towel and laid it across the sink. "But that doesn't mean I really dreamed about the victims before they were murdered."

"No." Her tone was matter-of-fact. "I have nothing but your word for that."

He leaned his hips against the counter and folded his arms across his chest. "There's only one way I can prove to you that my dreams are real."

Wariness flitted across her features. "How?"

"By capturing the killer."

"But you need my help to do that."

He nodded. "So deciding whether to work for me is a catch-22, isn't it?"

Her lips twisted upward in a cynical smile. "So what am I supposed to do, toss a coin?"

"I admit it's a crapshoot." He itched to kiss the smile off her face. "From your point of view, my story presents three possibilities."

"I've already mentioned one." She perched on the stool, propped her elbows on the counter and rested her chin on her clasped hands. "Even though these murders actually happened, you could have imagined your connection to them, maybe dreamed about them *after* the fact and confused the chronology.''

''The second possibility,'' he said, playing along, ''is that my story is true. That in some weird way I've established a psychic connection with the killer that tells me what he's thinking, planning.''

With raised eyebrows, he studied her, attempting to determine the impact of his words. She made no response, but stared past him out the kitchen window, as if searching for answers in the leafless trees.

His soft words broke the silence. ''Then there's the third possibility.''

''That *you're* the killer.'' She lifted her head, and her eyes, cool and dismal as a winter rain, confronted him.

His heart pounded in his throat. If she believed that, she would be lost to him forever. She might even report him to the authorities, who would ply him with questions he couldn't answer. Worst of all, she would think of him not as a man, but as a monster. But then, if she was seriously considering that, she wouldn't still be here.

''No...'' Her voice trailed off in the room's silence.

His hopes plummeted. ''I'm sorry, but I understand why you can't take the job.''

She shook her head, and her floral scent carried on the air currents. ''I'm not turning down the job.''

''But you said—''

''I said no, you're not a killer.''

Her smile, open and trusting, washed over him, and joy, an emotion he'd all but forgotten, bubbled up from obscurity. "What makes you so sure?"

She tapped her temple lightly. "When someone shot at me yesterday, you risked your life when you covered me with your body. Those aren't the actions of a killer."

It had been too long since anyone had shown such faith in him. No wonder he'd fallen in love with her in his dream. He was almost in love with her now. "That leaves only options one and two."

She grinned with an impishness that made her even more alluring. "Either you're telling the truth, or you're delusional. No matter which, the salary you're offering is too ridiculously extravagant for me to turn down."

HOURS LATER, TYLER FELT she'd earned every dime. Her neck and shoulders ached from long hours at the computer with little results, but she had no regrets about her decision to trust him. In the clear, gray light of morning, her fears had dissipated like mountain mist beneath the rising sun. He'd exhibited nothing but kindness, gentleness, and rash, heroic self-sacrifice when she'd been in danger. Delusional he might be, but Jared Slater would never harm her.

As soon as she had agreed to take the job, she'd tackled the task with enthusiasm. Jared had worked beside her, checking the information as she pulled it up on the screen, hoping to glimpse a name or fact to reveal the location of the next victim.

First, she eliminated all cities and towns with intersections of First and Orange except those in the Deep South where Spanish moss grew. That had left 143 possible locations.

"How can you narrow these down without visiting each of them?" she asked.

"The woman we're searching for lives in a three-story Victorian house," Jared said, "with azaleas around a broad front porch and wisteria growing over an arbor at the front gate of a picket fence."

She sighed with frustration. "That's half the houses in most of these towns."

"Then we've reached a dead end?" Alarm colored his words.

She massaged the aching muscles of her neck. "I'll check the National Registry of Historic Places on the chance the house is listed there."

Jared picked up the alphabetical list of 143 cities and towns. "I'll start at the top and call real-estate agents. I'll say I was driving through their area, and saw the house, and I'll describe it in complete detail. If I tell them it's the kind of property I want to purchase, maybe they'll recognize it."

All day, while she checked the registry and classified real-estate ads from newspapers in the target cities, Jared spoke with realtors and studied listings that hummed in over his fax line. None of the houses matched his dream.

Hours later, a dead end seemed no longer avoidable. "I don't know what else to try," she said.

He uttered a stream of curses that would have sent her well-bred grandmother into a swoon, then leaned back in his chair and closed his eyes. "I've seen that town a dozen times in my sleep. Turn-of-the-century buildings, moss-draped oaks overhanging the main street—"

"Names of businesses?" she prompted.

"Nope, nothing that helpful. Our only hope is the five realtors who were out when I called earlier today." He sat up and stretched, flexing his muscles with the lean power of a jungle cat. "I'll fix us some dinner, then hit the sack early. Maybe I'll dream something more specific tonight."

"Want some help in the kitchen?" She pushed away from the keyboard and stood, easing the cramps from her shoulders with a rolling motion. Her lips parted in surprise when strong hands grasped her from behind, massaging away the tension.

"You've done more than enough for one day." His warm breath skimmed her ear. "Sit down and give your mind a rest. There's usually a movie on TV this time of night."

She leaned back against the lean firmness of his chest, yielding to his warmth and strength, aching to kiss him, until the insistent buzz of the telephone brought her out of her reverie.

Jared took the loft stairs three at a time. When he answered the phone, she strained to hear over the loft wall.

She blushed at her eavesdropping. The call could be personal, nothing to do with their search, but her curiosity about every aspect of Jared's life was undeniable. However, her auditory snooping yielded nothing but Jared's murmured responses.

A few minutes later, he descended the stairs, clutching a legal pad. His grim expression unnerved her. "That was one of the realtors, returning my call."

"Another dead end?"

He shook his head. "The realtor said the house isn't for sale, but she recognized it. The owner's name is Evelyn Granger, and the house is located at the corner of First and Orange in Micanopy, Florida, south of Gainesville."

"So you've found her. That's good, isn't it?"

Agony lit his brown eyes with a golden light. "Only if she's still alive when we get there."

Chapter Five

Uttering a muffled curse, the stranger surfaced from a troubled sleep and groped for the telephone in the darkness of the motel room. "Yeah?"

"Your 4:00 a.m. wake-up call, sir," the desk clerk's cheery voice announced.

With effort, he threw back the tangled covers and reached for his pants. His joints groaned in protest and when he stood, his head throbbed with pain. His cold was no better, and he'd already lost a day.

"Fluids and aspirin," he mumbled before swallowing two tablets with a gulp of warm juice he'd purchased the previous evening from the motel vending machine. "Bed rest will have to come later."

He scowled, remembering his mother's adage: No rest for the wicked.

A forbidding figure stared back at him from the bathroom mirror, a man with tortured features and bloodshot eyes, who sported a two-day stubble streaked with silver. A man who'd forgotten how to smile.

Maybe he could smile again, once he'd taken care of Slater. But first, Slater had to suffer.

Dizziness assailed him, and he gripped the edge of the counter. Of all the damn stupid times to get sick. He leaned his burning forehead against the cool tile of the bathroom wall and waited for the giddiness to pass. His muscles ached and his knees trembled, objecting to his weight. At one time he could have crawled back to bed until his illness passed. Now he couldn't afford that luxury. There was too much to do, and time was running short.

Just let me finish the killing. Then I can die, for all I care.

Minutes later, he climbed into his Blazer and shivered in the predawn chill. The vending-machine coffee tasted horrible, but it helped drive his tremors away as he headed into the mountains. He had to kill Slater's girlfriend today, then he could rest until his sickness passed. When he was well again, he would take care of Slater.

Even with the heater pumping hot air, he shook with chills as he maneuvered the mountain curves. Each twist and turn made his stomach quiver. His headlights' high beams glanced off the mountain rock face, slick with moisture, rugged with cracks and crevices where the road had been blasted through. He clutched the steering wheel, forcing his blurring vision to pick out the white line that kept him on the highway.

Light-headed and aching, he turned at the church and ascended the road that led to Slater's. A flash of light on the mountain above warned him someone was coming down Slater's drive.

Cursing his luck, he backed into the driveway of an empty cottage, killed his lights, and waited. A few minutes later, a gray Volvo drove past. In the dawn twilight, he recognized the faces of the two people in the front seat. Jared Slater and the woman. But where the hell were they going at this hour of the morning?

He waited until they were well ahead of him, then threw the Blazer into gear and inched after them, easing without headlights down the shadowy road.

The two couldn't drive forever. He patted the bulk of the revolver in its holster beneath his arm. When they stopped, he would kill her.

JARED EASED THE VOLVO off the ramp into traffic streaming southwest on Interstate 85 toward Atlanta. "We should make good time, now that we're out of the mountains."

Tyler studied the map. "Even so, it'll take us about ten hours to reach Micanopy."

Jared nodded. "I think we'll arrive in time. I've had no dreams to indicate the killer is closing in yet."

She shifted uneasily against the restriction of the shoulder harness. Because he'd had no dreams, Jared had decided they had time to sleep last night—and to drive, rather than fly. According to Jared's accounts, he and the killer usually reached the crime scenes at the same time, but maybe in this instance, things would be different. Evelyn Granger would remain hale, whole and hearty, and Jared would admit that his dreams were delusions.

And she would be out of a job. The idea disturbed her—not because of the remarkable salary Jared was paying, but because she enjoyed being around him. Given enough time, she could fall in love with the guy's lean good looks, quirky humor and quick mind. Even his misguided inclination to help others had its charm.

Jared cast her a sideways glance before returning his attention to the road. "You still think I'm crazy, don't you?"

"Crazy is as crazy does," she said with an apologetic smile.

His face crinkled in a lopsided grin, creating a dimple in his cheek. "I guess this does seem like a wild-goose chase, heading south at the crack of dawn to track down a woman in a dream."

All morning, as Jared had steered the Volvo expertly along the mountain roads, questions about his story had niggled at her. "For the sake of argument," she said, "let's assume your premonitions are real."

"Isn't that why we're headed to Micanopy?"

"To either prove them or *disprove* them." She smiled to soften her correction. "But if you really are connected somehow to this killer's mind, what do you know about him?"

He pulled the Volvo into the passing lane and sped by an RV towing a compact car. "Not enough. I know he's eaten up with hatred and revenge."

She shuddered at the image. "You mean, you think he's a serial killer?"

His hands tightened on the steering wheel. "I don't think so. His victims aren't random. He seeks each one out purposely."

"Why?"

"Good question. If I knew the answer, I might know who he is."

If Jared was delusional, he was firmly entrenched in his madness. "Did you check to see if Veronica Molinsky and Mary Stanwick had anything in common?" she asked, hoping to illustrate the error of his thinking.

His answer surprised her. "Twenty years ago, when Pete Stanwick was a rookie detective, Larry Molinsky, Veronica's husband, worked as an assistant state's attorney in Stanwick's jurisdiction."

"They worked together?" If Jared was making all this up, his derangement displayed a remarkable creativity.

When the glare of the morning sun reflected off the back window of the car ahead, he removed his sunglasses from behind the visor and slipped them on. "That's the odd part. Pete Stanwick and Larry Molinsky collaborated on only one case, right before Molinsky moved to Washington."

His statements sounded so calm and reasoned, she almost forgot she was dealing with a man who claimed to see a killer in his dreams. "Does that case tie Mary Stanwick and Veronica Molinsky together somehow?"

He shook his head. "That was my first thought. But further investigation brought me to another dead end, literally."

"Another murder?" Her fear of his irrationality revived. The body count was growing too fast to believe.

He laughed with a sharp, barking snort. "That depends on your view of capital punishment."

The twists and turns of his logic eluded her. "What do you mean?"

He pulled the car into an exit lane, heading for a rest area. "I'm getting drowsy. I'll explain over a cup of coffee."

He parked between a minivan and an ancient Lincoln Town Car. Sunlight filtering through new leaves bathed the spring grass of the picnic area in dappled shade. In the thick woods surrounding the rest area, late dogwood and redbud blossomed, creating an atmosphere of serenity. A wren warbled in a nearby hedge. Thoughts of murder and killers didn't belong in such a place.

She lifted a basket from the rear seat and headed toward a picnic table beside a magnificent spirea, heavy with snowy flowers. As she removed a thermos, cups and cinnamon rolls from the basket, a black

Blazer caught her eye when it turned into a parking space on the other side of the rest rooms.

A memory niggled at her brain. The man at the Brevard service station had driven a Blazer. No one exited the car, and its tinted windshield shrouded the vehicle's occupants from view. She forced herself to breathe deeply and relax. Jared's crazy dreams had made her paranoid.

Jared poured himself a cup of coffee, bit into a sweet roll, and lounged on the concrete bench with one foot on the seat and an elbow propped on the table, studying her. "See someone you know?"

She shook her head and reached for the coffee. "Do you know anyone who owns a black Blazer?"

His scrutiny burned her as she selected a cinnamon bun and took a tentative bite. "No. Do you?"

"Uh-uh." She lowered her eyes to avoid his while she sipped her coffee.

"Then why does that Blazer have you spooked?"

"It doesn't."

He refused to relent. "In this instance, I don't have to be a psychic to read your mind. Your feelings are written all over your very attractive face."

His compliment barely registered. She didn't want to tell him about the man at the station. She didn't even want to think about the threats. "I'm just tired. We were up awfully early."

"Tiredness didn't drain the color from your cheeks." He gazed across the picnic tables at the

Blazer. "Maybe I ought to offer the driver some coffee."

As he started to rise, she grabbed his arm to hold him back. "No. It's nothing. All this talk of killing makes me nervous, that's all."

He cocked an eyebrow. "And that's why you're staring at that Blazer as if it's about to rush over here and attack you?"

Her laughter eased her tension. "It's not a big deal. When I stopped in Brevard before coming to your place, a man in a black Blazer warned me about you."

He set his cup down with a deliberate motion. "What did he say?"

She shivered, remembering. "That women around you keep turning up dead."

His gaze froze, cold and formidable. "He mentioned me by name?"

"Only after I asked if I was on the right road to your place." She wished she'd never brought up the subject. Fear and suspicion had driven the beauty out of the morning. As if to reflect her thoughts, a cloud drifted across the sun, casting the picnic area in gloom. "He was a mean-looking character, who probably never heard of you and just wanted to rattle a woman traveling alone."

The coldness in Jared's expression melted, and he reached out and hugged her to him. "Looks like he did a good job of that. But don't let it bother you. You'll notice dozens of black Blazers now. Remember how many white Broncos you saw after O.J.'s infamous ride?''

She groaned at the recollection. ''The trial of the century—and it seemed to last that long, too.''

She sat on the bench with Jared's arm comfortably draping her shoulder while she sipped her coffee. The easy companionship soothed her frazzled nerves. At the same time, the warmth of his body against hers generated a current of excitement and a heightened sense of anticipation deep in her abdomen. Unlike the men her grandmother had encouraged her to date— men from the "right" families—Jared Slater didn't treat her like a hothouse lily one minute, then try to wrestle her into his arms for a kiss and a feel, the next.

Not that the prospect of a little wrestling with him wasn't pleasant.

She reined in her fantasies and studied the black vehicle parked across the picnic area. Jared treated her like an equal, like an independent woman who knew her own mind. He hadn't pooh-poohed her fears about the Blazer. He, above all, understood the tricks the mind played.

''Speaking of trials,'' he said, ''I promised to tell you about the one Pete Stanwick and Larry Molinsky worked on.''

''Let me guess,'' she teased. ''It has to be a murder trial.''

''The worst kind.''

She grew solemn at the gravity in his voice. "How can one kind of murder be worse than another? Dead is dead."

His fingers tightened on her shoulder. "But some methods of dying are more horrible than others."

Overcast skies blocked the sun, turning the rest area into a secluded recess of shadows and silence. Hundreds of yards away, screened by thick hedges that muffled noise, cars and trucks whizzed by on the interstate. Beside her, Jared sat quietly, drawing circles in the red clay at their feet with a branch, as if reluctant to divulge the horror he'd discovered.

In spite of her jacket, she shivered in the light wind. She was no longer dealing with data on a computer printout but with the lives and deaths of real people. The anonymity of her computer terminal could not protect her from a killer who stalked the land, dispensing death according to some strange prescription only he understood. Whether Jared had really connected with this killer in his dreams didn't alter the fact that a murderer was out there, watching, waiting to strike again. If she and Jared could identify him, maybe other women wouldn't have to die.

Jared tossed the stick aside and stood, rammed his hands in his pockets and stared unseeingly past the busy lanes of traffic. "Twenty-seven years ago, a serial killer stalked women in Massachusetts. Not only did he commit murder, but he tortured his victims before they died."

This was no delusion. Jared sounded like a re-searcher who had done his homework. "And Pete Stanwick caught him?"

He nodded. "Stanwick had just been promoted to the criminal investigation division and partnered with Sam Witek, a twenty-year veteran of the force. To-gether the two of them tracked the murderer down, Ozzie Anderson, a dirt-poor day laborer with a psy-chotic hatred of women. Detectives Witek and Stan-wick gathered an ironclad case against Anderson, a whole truckload of irrefutable evidence."

She let him talk because he seemed to need to, but doubted that decades-old crimes had any relevance to the man they sought. "Where did Larry Molinsky fit in?"

"Molinsky was the prosecutor in the case."

"And he persuaded the jury to convict Ander-son?"

Jared poured himself more coffee and sat next to her. "Anderson never went to trial in Massachu-setts."

"Are you saying Ozzie Anderson is still out there, killing women?" Her alarm regenerated and her gaze flew to the Blazer, whose driver had yet to make an appearance.

He gave her knee a reassuring pat. "Relax and let me finish. In their investigations, Witek and Stan-wick tied Anderson not only to the Massachusetts murders but to several in New Jersey as well. They encouraged Molinsky to have Anderson extradited to stand trial in New Jersey."

"Why?"

"Because there was no death penalty in Massachusetts. They wanted to make sure Ozzie Anderson paid with his life for his crimes."

She quivered again in the early-morning breeze. "Let me guess. He was given a life sentence instead, let out on parole, and now for revenge, he's killing the wives of the men who caught him."

"Wrong." Jared loaded the thermos and cups into the basket and picked it up. "After twenty years of delays and appeals, Ozzie Anderson was finally executed by the state of New Jersey almost three years ago."

She followed him to the car. "Surely you're not suggesting the *ghost* of Ozzie Anderson is now wreaking its revenge?"

Jared placed the basket in the back seat, then turned to her with a rueful smile that accented the handsome lines of his face. "And you think *I'm* delusional?"

She shrugged, then slid onto the front seat as he held the door. "Makes about as much sense as anything else you've told me."

He leaned inside the car, his face inches from hers. All thoughts of murder and mayhem vanished in the gleaming light of his eyes and the scent of him—all spicy soap and leather—that filled her nostrils.

"It's elementary, Dr. Watson," he said with a wider grin that stirred butterflies in her stomach. "Ozzie

Anderson is a dead end, in more ways than one. There's either some other association between Mary Stanwick and Veronica Molinsky, or their connection through their husbands is simply a tragic coincidence.''

If she stared any longer into those deep brown eyes, she would do something on impulse she might later regret. To avoid his gaze, she pulled her shoulder harness taut and concentrated on the clasp at her hip. At the sound of her door closing, she expelled a sigh of relief. Seconds later, Jared climbed into the driver's seat and started the engine.

''Maybe Evelyn Granger's the key,'' she suggested, then blinked with surprise. If she truly believed anything concrete would result from his self-described wild-goose chase, she was as crazy as he was.

''If Evelyn knew both Mary and Veronica, then we'll know we're dealing with more than coincidence.'' He backed out, passed the parked Blazer, and drove onto the on-ramp, checking over his shoulder before entering the interstate.

She leaned against the headrest with closed eyes. She was losing her mind, buying into his story like this. Poor Evelyn Granger. Jared had pulled her name from a hat with his convoluted search for a Victorian house. All they would probably accomplish would be to scare the woman to death.

She heard Jared flick on the radio and a catchy country tune with improbable lyrics—something about a bad dog who gets no biscuit—filled the car.

The nonsensical words were as incongruous as her agreement to help Jared on his quest. He'd called her Dr. Watson. She felt more like Sancho Panza. The only difference was that Don Quixote's windmills never killed anyone.

She raised one eyelid and observed Jared's strong, slender fingers on the steering wheel, tapping in time to the music. Even his hands had character. Maybe that was why she felt so attracted to him. He might be crazy, but he had his principles and was willing to place himself at risk to help others.

She closed her eyes and pictured him in her mind— tall and slender, with latent power, lean and handsome features, and a shock of hair across his forehead that gave him a deceptively boyish look. Tall, dark, handsome—and probably nuts, into the bargain. What the hell had she gotten herself into?

"You asleep?"

Even his voice delighted her with its depth and timbre, sending a tingle through her. She opened her eyes and sat up. "With all that coffee in me, I'm wired for the next few hours. Want me to drive for a while?"

"Is your seat belt fastened?"

She detected a sense of urgency in his tone. "I fasten it automatically every time I get in a car. Why?"

He pressed the accelerator and the Volvo shot forward. "We're being followed."

She twisted in her seat and looked behind them. The front end of a black Blazer filled their rear windshield. With a burst of speed, the Volvo pulled away, but the Blazer soon caught up with them again.

Jared fixed his gaze on the road ahead. "He pulled out behind us when we left the rest area."

"He's been following us all this time?" Perspiration slicked her palms, and she wiped her hands on her jeans.

Jared gripped the wheel until his knuckles whitened, and set his handsome jaw into a hard line that caused a vein to pulse in his neck. "He hung back in the traffic. As soon as we left the other cars behind, he speeded onto our tail."

Her heart hammered in her throat and all the oxygen seemed squeezed from her lungs. "Maybe all he wants is to pass us," she said, not really believing it.

"I tried slowing down to let him around," Jared said between clenched teeth, "but he slowed, too."

She searched the highway ahead—a long, deserted stretch with trees in the median blocking the view of the oncoming traffic lanes. "Where's the highway patrol when you need them?"

"He's trying to pass," Jared said. "Maybe he'll keep going and leave us alone."

The needle on the speedometer dropped to eighty miles an hour as Jared eased off the accelerator, but they still hurtled like a bullet down the highway, and the countryside outside her window blurred. Tyler's feet pressed against the floorboard in an instinctive braking motion, and she gripped the edge of the seat as the Blazer veered toward them.

"My God!" she screamed. "He's going to hit us!"

As the Blazer slammed into the side of the Volvo, she screamed again. The force of the impact threw her against her seat belt, wrenching her shoulder and neck.

With superhuman strength, Jared held the car on the road, but the Blazer's driver didn't give up. Again he jerked the Blazer into the left side of the Volvo, shoving it into the emergency lane.

Her panic grew as the Volvo barreled along the shoulder. Gravel spat from beneath the wheels as Jared fought to bring the car under control. Its right wheels hit the edge of the pavement, jarring every bone in her body. In a few seconds of deadly silence, the road noise ceased as the Volvo lifted off the ground and rotated in the air.

They were both going to die.

She strained against her shoulder harness as the car catapulted, and the world turned upside down. When the car crashed onto its roof, her seat belt yanked her back into her seat, and the air bags inflated, enfolding her in darkness.

Chapter Six

Smothering darkness, penetrated by horrible, cackling cries that made his skin crawl, engulfed Jared. He'd seen pictures of hell, but he'd never imagined what it sounded like. Gradually the blackness lifted, and a cushion of crushed grass vibrated beneath him as vehicles thundered past. He wasn't dead, after all.

Then the stench hit him, and his stomach recoiled with nausea.

"Take it easy, son," a man's voice drawled. "Help's on the way."

Jared opened his eyes to see a tanned leather face set with brilliant blue eyes beneath the brim of a battered straw hat. A blinding, pulsating glare surrounded the hat like a shining crown.

Jared squeezed his eyes shut, fearful that his visual hallucinations had returned. When he opened them again, the man, dressed in faded overalls and a flannel shirt, stepped from between him and the bright morning sun and knelt beside him. His sunlit halo disappeared, but fluttering bits of white filled the air. Snow again, in May?

With his aching head pounding in protest, Jared propped himself on his elbows in the grass, and his memory of the crash returned in a rush. Panic and a terrible foreboding surged through him. "Tyler?"

The man's hand on his shoulder prevented him from rising. "Your lady friend's fine. She's in that fancy car over there, calling the police."

Jared sagged back to the ground with relief. His glance slid down the roadside past a dark blue Lexus to a gully beyond where his Volvo—or what was left of it—rested.

His rescuer followed his gaze. "I was coming up behind you in the inside lane and saw that feller smash into you. You'd have been okay if you hadn't hit the edge. Flipped your car right off the road and rolled you down the embankment."

The impact had crushed the roof and sides of the Volvo like a tin can in a trash compactor. If he and Tyler had been in a less sturdy vehicle, they would both be dead.

Jared flexed his fingers and toes, and their quick response reassured him. Aside from a splitting headache and terrible nausea from the overpowering odor, he seemed okay.

Checking in the opposite direction, he discovered the source of the stench and noise. His rescuer was evidently a chicken farmer on his way to market. In a dilapidated truck, piled high with crates, cackling hens beat their wings against the cages, filling the air with a storm of white feathers and a smell that would choke a goat.

Jared waved away the farmer's outstretched hand and hefted himself to a sitting position. ''Did you get the Blazer's license number?''

''Sorry, his plate was so muddy, I couldn't even tell what state he was from.'' The farmer pushed back his hat, and the sun beat on his reddened skin. ''Whoever he was, he's a bad 'un. Didn't slow down one stitch when you went off the road. Just took off like a bat out of hell.''

''Jared, are you all right?'' Tyler hurried toward him and knelt in the lush grass, her gray eyes wide with worry. Unfamiliar emotion flooded him at the sight of her—or maybe the strange sensations her presence conjured in the pit of his stomach were simply an aftermath of his blow to the head, which throbbed so painfully he couldn't think straight.

She sat back on her heels and scrutinized him with anxious eyes. ''You were knocked out, and I was afraid the car might explode before I could pull you away. Thank God, Mr. McCracken stopped and helped.''

The farmer's reddened face darkened at her praise. ''Just being neighborly, miss. Anybody in these parts would do the same.''

Tyler jerked her head toward the Lexus. ''She's on her way to a convention in Atlanta, but she stopped to call for help on her car phone. The highway patrol and an ambulance should be here soon.''

''No need for an ambulance—'' Jared nodded toward the Volvo and grimaced ''—but we could use a tow truck. And it looks like I'll be needing new air bags.''

''You might as well have a new car built around them.'' Tyler grinned shakily. ''I'm amazed we both got out alive.''

Above the rumble of speeding traffic, approaching sirens pierced the cool morning air, and on the highway behind them, two Georgia Highway Patrol cars crested the rise.

Jared shoved himself to his feet, fighting dizziness. ''Was I unconscious long?''

''Not long,'' she assured him, ''but it seemed like forever.''

Her concern touched him, and he cursed himself for a fool. If she'd been hurt, he would be the one to blame. He should have heeded the warning in his dreams and sent her away as soon as the ice melted. He'd persuaded himself he needed her help to save Evelyn Granger, but what he really wanted was to keep her beside him for as long as he could. His selfishness could have been the death of her.

The patrol cars pulled off the road, crushing a blanket of dandelions and clover beneath their heavy-duty tires, and parked with lights still flashing. A heavy-set trooper in a freshly pressed uniform exited the first car and approached. ''What happened here?''

"A black Blazer followed us out of the last rest area," Jared said. Relying on concise journalistic style, he provided the salient details. He'd barely finished his story when more sirens sounded.

"That'll be the ambulance," the trooper said.

Jared tried to ignore the pummeling in his temples. "We're okay—"

"We'll let the doctors be the judge of that," the trooper replied in a tone that discouraged dissent. "EMS will take you to the emergency room in Commerce. I'll meet you there when we've finished our investigation here."

FOUR HOURS LATER, Jared paced the worn linoleum of the hospital corridor. The harsh fluorescent lights and cloying antiseptic smells recalled memories of another hospital two years ago.

He stopped, pressed his aching forehead against the wall's cool plaster, and squeezed his eyelids shut against the unwelcome recollection, but his mind's eye relayed bright and clear the image of a stocky man in his thirties, with thinning blond hair and eyes the color of faded denim, clutching a filthy, blood-soaked towel to his face. Jared had been wondering who or what had inflicted the jagged wound that laid open the man's cheek, when pain had exploded in his head, obscuring his vision like torrents of crimson rain in the instant before he'd lost consciousness.

A tremor of superstition shook him before he shrugged off his irrational fear of hospitals and resumed pacing and waiting for Tyler. He hadn't had a moment alone with her since the accident. An EMS technician had monitored their blood pressure and pulse during the ambulance ride to the hospital.

There they had been shunted to separate cubicles to await examination. After the doctor had proclaimed Jared fit for release, the trooper had corralled him to finish his interrogation. Tyler was secluded with the trooper now, providing her version of events.

Jared prayed she wouldn't reveal his strange dreams. He couldn't help her or Evelyn Granger if he was locked up in the loony bin. And God only knew what the trooper would conclude if she told him of the Blazer driver's warning that women around Jared kept turning up dead.

Tyler had obviously had good reason to be frightened of the Blazer driver. Probably he was some sicko who had attached himself to Tyler after encountering her at the service station. After all, with her flawless complexion, luxuriant hair and appealing figure, she was a striking woman. As he'd discovered in an investigative piece he'd written on stalkers several years ago, men who hated women and flaunted power over them often chose the prettiest ones as their victims.

He sank onto a vinyl-covered sofa in the waiting area and cradled his aching head in his hands, waiting for the Tylenol the doctor had given him to kick in. If only he'd managed to glimpse the driver through the Blazer's tinted windows, maybe he would have been able to give the police a description.

A disturbing thought joined the pounding in his brain, turning his blood cold. Maybe, since he had some psychic connection with the man who killed Stanwick and Molinsky, the killer also perceived his thoughts. If that was the case, he knew Jared was on his trail and might do anything to stop him—like taking a shot at him on the mountaintop or trying to run him off the road.

The Blazer driver's cryptic warning to Tyler now assumed new and deadly meaning, especially if the deceased women he'd alluded to were Mary Stanwick and Veronica Molinsky.

Jared slammed a fist into his palm and cursed his own stupidity. If the man in the Blazer was the killer he sought, Tyler was in even worse danger than he'd realized.

"ARE YOU SURE YOU DON'T want me to drive?" Tyler asked as they approached the interstate.

Jared shook his head. "I'm fine. My headache's almost gone."

She touched her face testily, fingering the bruise that had formed on her right cheekbone. "We were both lucky, but I'm sorry about your car."

He patted the steering wheel. "The rental car will do until the insurance company evaluates the Volvo. And whoever was driving the Blazer won't be looking for us in a Ford Taurus."

She tried to block the stranger's intimidating face from her memory. He was somewhere out there, maybe searching for them this very minute. Before they left the hospital, the highway patrolman had advised them the Blazer had been found abandoned, wiped clean of prints and any other identification. That car, too, had been a rental, but a trace of the credit card it was charged to had turned up a false ID.

"Do you think he's still after us?" she asked.

Jared shrugged and kept his eyes on the road. "I can't be concerned with him now. He's already taken a six-hour chunk out of our time, and I have to reach Evelyn Granger to warn her."

She bit her lip and tamped down her exasperation. Jared was ignoring the real threat of the Blazer driver to chase after threats he'd only dreamed about. But she shouldn't be surprised. She'd known he was irrational from the moment they'd met, but she'd been desperate for the job he'd offered, and, in her best Florence Nightingale mode, hoped the trip to Florida would convince him of his delusions and encourage him to seek help.

What she hadn't counted on was meeting a homicidal maniac at a service station. Had the man really stalked her across three states?

Jared interrupted her thoughts. "What did you tell them?"

"Who?"

"The highway patrol." His casual tone belied the tension in his body as he waited for her answer.

She stretched and rolled her head on her shoulders, hoping to alleviate the tightness in her neck and shoulders, remnants of the crash. "What could I tell them? A car ran us off the road. It could have been the same car I saw two days ago, but I didn't see the driver who hit us, so I can't be sure."

"Anything else?"

"Of course." She bristled at his interrogation. She'd suffered enough grilling from the Georgia Highway Patrol. "I explained we were in a dreadful hurry to reach Florida to warn a woman whom you'd seen murdered in your dreams."

"Holy—" Jared struck the steering wheel with the palm of his hand and filled the car with oaths, some more original than others. His wealth of blue vocabulary amazed her. Must be the writer in him.

She waited until he had exhausted his repertoire of curses. "Don't you know sarcasm when you hear it? Of course, I didn't tell them about your dreams. I didn't want them thinking we were *both*—"

She paused, searching for a delicate way to phrase it.

"Crazy?" he supplied.

She nodded and eyed him anxiously, wondering if his anger had passed.

The tension drained from his body and he slumped against the seat. "I'm sorry. I should have known you wouldn't say anything, but—"

"What could I say? Your dream story is so beyond bizarre, I'd sound insane just repeating it." She placed her hand on his arm to soften her accusation. "Besides, you've never dreamed about the guy in the Blazer, right?''

"Not that I know of.''

"Then there was no reason for me to mention your dreams to the highway patrol.'' She didn't blame him for being edgy. Although he believed in his dreams, he realized how others would view them.

"Hungry?'' he asked.

She relaxed at the change of subject. "Not until the butterflies finish their aerial show in my stomach. It hasn't stopped rolling since the car did.''

He threw her a searching look. "Maybe you'll feel like eating by the time we reach the airport.''

Jared Slater presented her with one surprise after another. "Airport? To reach the airport, we'll have to take the interstate through downtown Atlanta. I thought you were in a hurry.''

"This won't take long.''

"*What* won't take long?''

"Putting you on a plane to Asheville,'' he said in an intractable tone. "You can pick up a rental car there to drive to my place, then switch to your car and go home.''

"Are you out of your mind?'' she sputtered, then winced at her choice of words.

Jared didn't blink, but his jaw tensed and a vein pulsed noticeably in his throat. "I was crazy to risk bringing you with me. I've put you in terrible danger.''

She raked her fingers raggedly through her hair. "And you think dumping me off in the middle of nowhere will make me safer?"

A smile quirked the corner of his mouth. "Atlanta's hardly the middle of nowhere. You've heard that old Southern joke—even if you're going straight to hell, you have to change planes in Atlanta."

The man was definitely certifiable. "You can laugh, Jared Slater, because that maniac in the black Blazer isn't after you."

His smile faded. "I never said he was."

"Then how can you be sure he isn't after *me?* That he didn't pick me out as his victim when he first saw me in Brevard?" She twisted as far toward him as her shoulder harness allowed. "How can you be sure he hasn't gone back to your place to wait for our return?"

He wasn't deterred. "Then I'll buy you a ticket for Raleigh-Durham. Your grandmother can pick you up, and I'll have your car delivered to you when I return from Florida."

She collapsed against the seat, not knowing which was worse—driving to Florida with a crazy man or returning home to Gran's incessant I-told-you-so's.

Not to mention that she'd become overly fond of the kooky but desirable man next to her. She hadn't realized how fond until she'd seen his unconscious body, dangling from the shoulder harness of the Volvo, and her heart had constricted with grief. Now the thought of not seeing him again, of allowing him to continue suffering his delusions with no one to convince him to seek help, filled her with an incredible sadness.

If she could persuade him to let her tag along long enough to prove his dreams were deceptive, maybe he would forget about sending her away. Under no circumstances would she return to the mountaintop alone with the dark stranger after her. Nor would she admit defeat by running home to Gran and dependence.

"Look—" she employed her most patient tone "—you admitted the man won't recognize our car. If he has no idea where we're headed, I'm perfectly safe."

"But what if he does know?" A sense of urgency underlaid his words.

She threw up her hands in exasperation. "How could he know?"

He glanced toward her again, and she recoiled at the pain in his eyes.

"You still don't believe my claims about my dreams, do you?"

Her heart softened at his distress. "I believe *you* believe them."

"So you're tagging along to play nursemaid to your poor, misguided, crazy boss." He ground out the words between gritted teeth.

Unsure how to respond, she took a deep breath and studied the passing landscape while she cast about for a reply. "I just want to do the job you hired me to do."

She tensed at the sight of the approaching interchange. Ahead traffic split in one direction toward downtown Atlanta, in the other toward the beltline that by-passed the city. She held her breath as Jared pressed the accelerator, then switched into the bypass lane.

"You're not sending me home?" she asked in amazement.

He reached over, brushed her cheek with his knuckles, and threw her an achingly attractive smile. "I'm the crazy one, remember?"

MAYBE HE *WAS* CRAZY, Jared thought as he flipped on the lights in the suite of the Residence Inn outside Gainesville and dumped their suitcases at the foot of the loft stairs. Maybe his mountain isolation had driven him over the edge and he didn't even know it. Otherwise, what the hell was he doing, six hundred miles from home at midnight in a strange motel, placing an incredibly beautiful and caring woman in mortal danger, all because of some damn dream?

Tyler glanced around the room. He followed her gaze, taking in the kitchen, sitting area, dining room, and the stairs to the loft bedroom. The contemporary furniture and carpets in soothing sea greens and blues provided a welcome change from the bleak darkness he'd driven through for the past six hours.

"Where do I sleep?" she asked.

He nodded toward the loft bedroom, picked up her bag, and started up the stairs.

She laid a restraining hand on his arm. "Then where do you sleep?"

He suppressed a grin at the suspicion sparking her cool gray eyes. "Downstairs."

She eyed the cozy love seats skeptically. "On one of those?"

He set down her bags, stepped around to the dining-area wall, and pulled a handle. A wide Murphy bed unfolded. "All the comforts of home."

His eyes met hers, and for an instant, an intriguing warmth ignited her gaze the way heat lightning backlighted clouds in the night sky, arousing a corresponding glow deep in his abdomen. An overwhelming desire to embrace her and tumble both of them into the soft depths of the Murphy bed seized him.

He shoved the bed into the wall with an emphatic thud. She already believed he was crazy. No need for her to think him a sex maniac, as well.

"Aren't you tired?" she asked.

"Sure, but I think I'll take a shower before turning in." A very cold shower.

"Thanks for not sending me away. You won't regret it." She stretched up on tiptoe and planted a tentative kiss on his cheek, then grabbed her bag and rushed up the stairs.

Hell, he already regretted it. His only hope was to identify the killer before he could harm Evelyn Granger. Only then would Tyler be safe, as well.

Hours later, he jolted from a deep sleep with a tortured scream on his lips. Above him, a light switched on in the loft, and before he could reach for his robe, footsteps pattered down the stairs.

"Are you okay?"

Tyler stood over him, the light from the stairwell outlining her alluring silhouette through the sheer cotton of her short gown. Her hand cupped his forehead as if she was feeling for fever, and he leaned into the comfort of her touch as he struggled to regain his breath and calm his pounding heart.

She settled on the edge of the bed, and he grasped her hands in his, hoping the contact would drive the residual horrors from his mind.

Her fingers rested on his wrist. "Your pulse is galloping. Another dream?"

The faint light illuminated the delicate profile of her face and the soft wing of hair that covered one cheek. God, she was so beautiful and so brave. After all she'd been through the past few days, she still managed to radiate calmness and poise.

He'd had another dream, all right, but he hesitated to tell her. She already seemed convinced he was a lunatic. Now the only way to convince her he was sane and to guarantee her safety was to catch the killer.

"Yes," he said, finally drawing breath enough to speak. "The killer's closing in on Evelyn Granger. We don't have much time."

Chapter Seven

Jared left the stream of traffic headed toward Walt Disney World, turned off the interstate at Exit 73, and headed east into the rising sun toward Micanopy.

Tyler inhaled deeply as the car's air conditioner churned out cold, crisp air, a welcome contrast to the muggy atmosphere that had enveloped them when they'd stepped out of the suite into the feeble dawn light. But even deep breathing couldn't calm her this morning. She was not looking forward to their encounter with Evelyn Granger.

She smoothed the short skirt of her cotton floral dress, thankful she'd remembered to pack cool clothes in spite of the melting snow they'd left behind in the Smokies. Strange, how just a few hundred miles could produce such contrasts—from rugged mountain passes to rolling hills of Georgia clay, to wetlands thick with cypress and live oaks bearded with flowing manes of grizzled Spanish moss.

The one bright spot in her morning was the knowledge that the stranger who had run them off the road yesterday wouldn't find them here. The highway, a winding country road, seemed abandoned after the interstate's heavy traffic, but the peaceful, pastoral landscape of wide meadows interspersed with stands of slash pine and groves of ancient oaks provided little relief from her agitation.

Her uneasiness had begun when Jared's scream awakened her from a sound sleep. She'd stumbled down the stairs to find him sitting upright in bed, gasping for air. A fine sheen of perspiration covered his bare chest, a sight that had sent her heart skipping and her palms itching to caress his smooth muscles.

His eyes glowed feverishly, and she'd felt his forehead and checked his pulse, fearful he was ill. Although his heart raced faster than her own, he wasn't sick, but was suffering the aftermath of another nightmare. She'd longed to wrap her arms around him to ease his torment, but his impatience had curbed her desire.

After urging her to dress, he'd hustled her to the car without breakfast in his haste to reach Evelyn Granger. Now, alternating sun and shade played like a strobe light across the rigid planes of his face as the car passed beneath the trees that overhung the road. Except for a vertical crease between his dark eyebrows, his stoic expression gave no hint of his urgency.

"Do you have a plan?" she asked.

He started, as if roused from a sound sleep. "For what?"

She sighed with frustration. It was possible that she'd met the man of her dreams, but *his* dreams were making her crazy. His insistence on the validity of his wacko fantasies placed him on a fast track to the nut house—not to mention that he was prepared to scare an unsuspecting woman senseless in the process.

She struggled to keep the irritation from her voice. "You can't just walk up to Evelyn Granger with an 'Excuse me, but I believe there's a killer out to get you.'"

"I'll think of something."

He flashed her a lopsided smile that reminded her why she stayed with him, in spite of his delusions. Handsome, intelligent, compassionate. Did those qualities cancel out lunacy, or was *she* the insane one?

"Please," she begged, "why frighten the woman? Why don't we just hang around and keep an eye on her?"

He shot her a withering glance. "Because I couldn't live with myself if that monster comes after her and I didn't at least try to warn her."

Stark, staring crazy, that's what he was. And the sexiest, most fascinating man she'd ever met. One thing she had to admit—working for Jared Slater was anything but dull.

"Okay—" She decided on a delaying tactic. "How about some breakfast? I'm starving, and I doubt Evelyn Granger's even awake yet."

When they entered the main street of Micanopy, the quaint turn-of-the-century brick buildings and canopied oaks that shaded the wide street provided a setting ill-suited for murder. A scruffy yellow dog, scratching halfheartedly, lay in a puddle of sunlight outside the Wild Flowers Café. He lifted his head with an inquisitive glance as they climbed out of the car, wagged his tail lazily, then laid his head on his giant paws and scrutinized them as they entered the restaurant.

In contrast to the empty streets, the café was packed with people mingling among the tables, calling greetings and joking with each other by first names, like folks who'd known one another for a lifetime. Sunlight glinted off multiple panels of decorative stained glass that adorned the walls and windows, and the heady aromas of brewed coffee, sizzling bacon and fresh bread made Tyler's mouth water.

She contemplated the congenial surroundings with a surge of hope. Maybe the relaxing atmosphere of the sleepy town and interaction with the friendly townspeople would calm Jared's fevered dreams. It was possible the dreams were a result of his self-enforced exile on his lonely mountaintop. Besides, she wouldn't mind staying here awhile. The tiny village, off the usual roads traveled by tourists and residents alike, provided a perfect hiding place from the demented Blazer driver.

"Over there." Jared pointed to a table by the front window and guided her by the elbow through the crowded room.

"You folks want coffee?" A waitress, sporting a teased coiffure of red-orange hair with gray roots, filled their cups from a glass carafe. "I'll be back for your orders in a minute."

"Where can we find Seminole Properties?" Jared flashed the woman an appealing grin.

The waitress countered with a flirtatious smile and patted her lacquered hair. "For you, mister, I'll *bring* you Seminole Properties."

She threaded her way between tables to a corner where a middle-aged woman sat, reading the Gainesville *Sun.* Wearing a burgundy business suit with a candy-striped blouse, she seemed overdressed compared to the rest of the café's clientele. When the waitress spoke with a jerk of her head toward the window table, the woman folded her newspaper, tucked it beneath her arm, and crossed the room. Even her walk was businesslike.

The rosy cheeks of her plump face dimpled as she smiled and nodded, causing a slight bounce of her salt-and-pepper curls. "I'm Bobbie Hendrix, owner of Seminole Properties. What can I do for you?"

Jared had shoved himself to his feet at her approach. After introducing himself and Tyler, he indicated an empty chair at the table. "Join us?"

Bobbie took a seat, and the waitress reappeared with another cup and the coffee carafe.

"Jared Slater." Bobbie's eyes lighted with recognition. "Didn't I speak with you on the phone a couple of days ago?"

"I'm interested in an old Victorian house," Jared acknowledged. "You said you had one here in town that fits my description."

Tyler stared out the window, holding her breath and praying Jared wouldn't divulge his crazy dreams.

Bobbie's pleasant expression crumpled. "You've driven all this way for nothing. Evelyn Granger's house isn't for sale. I thought I made that clear on the telephone."

"You did," Jared said, "but we'd like to speak with Mrs. Granger anyway."

Bobbie shrugged. "It won't do you much good. Evelyn's lived in that house over forty years. Came here as a bride, raised three children, buried her husband—all from that house. She isn't about to sell."

Tyler's appetite suddenly waned. If Evelyn Granger had lived forty years in Micanopy, a town as forgotten by time as Brigadoon, the likelihood of her connection with Stanwick and Molinsky diminished. And that meant Jared Slater was as crazy as she'd feared.

Jared leaned toward Bobbie, his expression a mixture of charm and embarrassment. "You misunderstand. My fiancée—"

Tyler's eyes widened when he reached across the table and clasped her hand, squeezing it playfully.

"—and I," Jared continued, "just want to see the house. We'll describe it to our architect and have him build a reproduction, since the original's unavailable."

Bobbie's eyes narrowed with suspicion. "I thought you knew what it looked like. After all, you described it to me."

"We only know the outside," Tyler blurted, anxious to speak before Jared revealed his visions. "I've always dreamed of a house like this—maybe I saw a picture as a child. And then, one day, while passing through, we saw Mrs. Granger's home. But if we're going to build one, we'll need some idea of the interior layout."

Bobbie relaxed and took a sip of coffee. Maybe she was accustomed to off-the-wall requests in her business. "Guess it won't hurt for you to ask Evelyn. She should be opening in about an hour."

"Opening?" Jared asked.

"Evelyn operates Precious Memories Antiques and Collectibles in the next block. The shop opens at nine." Bobbie rose and handed Jared a business card. "And if you run into a dead end with Evelyn, give me a call. I have a few other Victorians that might interest you."

Jared watched the realtor return to her corner table and unfold her paper, then turned to Tyler with a tormented look. "A dead end is exactly what I'm trying to prevent."

A FEW MINUTES AFTER nine, sated with a Belgian waffle topped with whipped cream and fresh blueberries, Tyler trotted to keep up with Jared's long strides as he crossed the main street and headed down the block.

She was the one who needed her head examined for going along with Jared. Once he began spouting his strange tales, Evelyn Granger would probably scream for the men in the little white coats. Tyler wondered if there was such a charge as "insanity by association."

She was beginning to suspect she really was losing her mind. As they covered the block to Precious Memories, she experienced an eerie feeling of déjà vu, of having walked this same street before. Everything seemed familiar, but she'd never been to Micanopy. The closest she'd come was eleven years ago when she and her grandmother had barreled past on the interstate toward Orlando and Walt Disney World.

A bell tinkled above the shop door as Jared opened it for her, and they stepped into a huge store with high ceilings, crammed baseboard to crown molding with every form of antique and collectible imaginable. Glass cases displayed Art Deco costume jewelry, Victorian beaded bags and railroad pocket watches.

Row after row of Chippendale and Hepplewhite butted clawed feet and finials with monstrous Victorian bedsteads and armoires. China bowls of potpourri were scattered throughout the store, mingling the fragrance of roses and lavender with the musty smell of age. In a rear corner, a human skeleton hung from a metal stand beside a cupboard of grotesque surgical implements and bottles of patent medicines.

A tiny woman, frail and birdlike, stepped from behind a counter. "You folks looking for something in particular, or just browsing?"

"Mrs. Granger?" Jared asked.

The woman nodded with a look of surprise, and Tyler's stomach twisted at the prospect of scaring the fragile old lady with Jared's horrid nightmares.

"Roseville pottery," Tyler exclaimed in an attempt to forestall Jared's disclosures. "I'm looking for a nice addition to my grandmother's collection."

Fearful of his reaction, she averted her eyes from Jared.

"I have several excellent pieces." Mrs. Granger waved a hand gnarled with arthritis toward the window, where a set of low shelves displayed a variety of vases in muted shades of pink, blue, and green.

"They're lovely," Tyler murmured, all too aware of Jared's annoyed look. He observed her with his hands shoved in his back pockets and his eyebrows elevated above impatient eyes. Tension crackled from his muscles. They were coiled like a jungle cat's, ready to spring.

"These make *me* feel like an antique," Mrs. Granger said with a pleasant laugh. "When I was a girl, my mother could buy these at the five-and-dime for a little over a dollar. This piece—" she selected a blue vase with a raised motif of white magnolia blossoms "—sells for three hundred dollars now."

"We'll take it." Jared withdrew his wallet and extracted his charge card. His smile, subdued yet challenging, weakened Tyler's knees. "I'm sure your grandmother will love it."

She opened her mouth to protest, then clamped it shut, sensing her refusal would only make matters worse.

Mrs. Granger nodded toward the street. "Traffic is picking up now. I'll be busier than a one-armed paperhanger by noon."

Grateful to pursue any subject other than Jared's dreams, Tyler plunged into conversation. "Micanopy is so isolated. How do people find this place?"

"It was a well-kept Florida secret until the movie came out." Mrs. Granger punched Jared's account number into her credit-card machine.

"Movie?" Jared asked in a tone more impatient than curious.

"*Doc Hollywood,* with Michael J. Fox." Mrs. Granger returned his card and began to wrap the vase in tissue paper. "Business has boomed ever since they used our town for a location."

Tyler heaved an inward sigh of relief. Her déjà vu hadn't been an indication she was going bonkers. She'd seen the movie twice—once at the theater and later on television. No wonder the street seemed familiar.

Her relief was short-lived.

"I have a confession to make." Jared accepted the padded bundle from Mrs. Granger. "We didn't really come here to buy antiques."

"But you did." The little woman nodded toward the vase swathed in newspaper and graced him with a gentle smile. "And I thank you for your business."

The bell tinkled behind them, and a couple, clad in shorts, tank tops and thong sandals and glowing with sunburn, entered the store.

"Jeez, look at all the Carnival glass, George." The woman's Brooklyn accent grated on Tyler's Southern ears, but George didn't reply. He headed toward the back of the store and a display of antique tools.

Tyler placed her hand on Jared's arm. "Maybe we should be going."

Jared ignored her. "I must talk with you, Mrs. Granger. It's urgent."

A low growl erupted at Tyler's feet, where a Pekingese planted itself in front of Mrs. Granger and bared its teeth at Jared.

"It's all right, Buffy," Mrs. Granger crooned. "Go back to your bed." She shooed the tiny dog behind the counter and turned to Jared. "Once I wait on these other folks, I'll be happy to talk with you."

Tyler assessed the cluttered shop, wondering if she could pull Mrs. Granger aside and assure her that Jared was harmless, but speaking with the woman without Jared overhearing appeared impossible.

Faced with the inevitability of Jared's disclosure, she seized her only other choice. "I'll wait for you outside."

Without lingering for his reply, she hurried out onto the street.

Damn Jared Slater's crazy dreams. He shouldn't use them as an excuse to terrorize sweet little old ladies like Mrs. Granger. If Tyler intended to continue working for him, she had to convince him to seek professional help.

ONCE THE OTHER CUSTOMERS had left the shop, Evelyn Granger turned to Jared. "Now, young man, what did you wish to speak with me about?"

A trickle of nervous perspiration slid down his spine. He had to sound convincing. Her life depended on it. "I'm a reporter—"

"How nice." Her pleasant smile lit her face. "And you want to do a feature on my shop?"

He shook his head. "I'm an investigative reporter. I'm trying to track down a murderer."

"What does that have to do with me?" Her bewildered tone caused the Pekingese to stand in its bed behind the counter and issue a threatening snarl.

Jared rubbed the back of his neck as he searched for the right words. "In my investigation, I've come across evidence that this killer is after you."

"Me?" Her trilling laugh echoed in the store. "You must be mistaken. I don't have an enemy in the world."

"I'm sure that's what Mary Stanwick and Veronica Molinsky thought." He watched her face for signs of recognition, but all he found was puzzlement.

"Do they live around here?" she asked.

"Mary Stanwick lived in Massachusetts, Veronica Molinsky in Washington, D.C."

She shrugged. "Then I wouldn't know them. I grew up in New York and moved here as a bride."

Her disbelief was obvious, and his desperation grew. "You have to believe me, Mrs. Granger. You are on this killer's hit list."

Her eyes narrowed, appraising him. "Who is this killer?"

"We don't know his name." He avoided her eyes.

She shook her head sadly. "Then how can you possibly know he's after me?"

"Through sources that I can't divulge." His heart sank at the continued skepticism in her expression. "Promise me that you'll be careful, Mrs. Granger. Lock your doors and don't go out at night alone."

She reached across the counter and patted his hand. A kind sympathy shone in her eyes. "I'm always careful. Now, why don't you go find that nice young woman who was with you earlier?"

She retreated to the back of the shop, and when Jared started to follow, the Pekingese barred his way.

TYLER AMBLED AIMLESSLY along the street, window-shopping at stores that sold books, cameos and hand-crafted items. She passed an antique store that specialized in Depression glass and Florida citrus-crate labels. When she turned back toward Mrs. Granger's shop, Jared stepped out, and she hurried to meet him.

"Come on." He grasped her elbow and led her at a fast pace toward the car.

Tyler glanced over her shoulder, trying to catch a glimpse of Mrs. Granger through the shop window. "What did you tell her?"

Jared didn't break his stride. "That in my work as an investigative reporter I'd come across information that someone was out to kill her."

Tyler stopped in the middle of the sleepy street. "And she believed you?"

His bitter chuckle echoed in the empty space. "She laughed at me. Said she doesn't have an enemy in the world and that I must have mistaken her for someone else."

"Did she know Mary Stanwick or Veronica Molinsky?"

Jared shook his head. "Never heard of them."

"And that was it?"

"I tried to persuade her." He spoke through gritted teeth. "She just patted my hand—it was obvious she thought I was a nut case."

At least he hadn't frightened the poor woman. "Then our work here is finished."

"Finished?" He continued toward the car. "Our work's just begun. Since Evelyn Granger won't be on guard, we'll have to stand watch for her."

Tyler groaned. Jared's porch light might be burning, but there was definitely nobody home. She consoled herself with a reminder of how much he was paying her for this nonsense. And with the fact that he fascinated her.

"I'm a researcher," she insisted, "not a bodyguard."

He opened the door of the Taurus for her. "Researchers search for things, right?"

"Of course." She slid onto the seat and took the Roseville vase from him.

He leaned into the car, his face inches from hers. The sincerity in his intent brown eyes gave no hint of dementia. "Then, as my research assistant, your job is to help me find a killer."

THE DIGITAL CLOCK beside the bed glowed 2:00 a.m. Using the dregs of her energy, Tyler stripped off her clothes, shrugged on her nightgown and fell across the comfortable king-size bed at the Residence Inn. She was accustomed to long hours at the computer or prowling through library stacks and files, but surveilling little old ladies was out of her area of expertise— and more exhausting.

Jared had insisted they remain in Micanopy's business district until Mrs. Granger closed her shop for the day. They'd whiled away hours browsing through the shops, eating lunch at a window table at the Wild Flowers Café and ice cream afterward on a shaded bench across from Precious Memories. When Mrs. Granger closed at five o'clock, they'd followed her home. Jared had circled the block a few times, then parked near a wooded lot down the street from the Victorian house, and they had waited.

Twilight had fallen. Jared switched off the air conditioner and rolled down the window. Cicadas and the plaintive hoot of a screech owl broke the stillness. In the intimacy of the car, surrounded by darkness broken only by a dim streetlight at Mrs. Granger's corner, Tyler studied the man beside her.

She had taken a risk in continuing to work for him, and until now she hadn't examined her motives too closely. Maybe she'd been afraid of what she would find. Sure, she had wanted to be independent of Gran, but her reason for staying with Jared went deeper than a need for freedom.

From the moment she'd met him, his deep-seated integrity had drawn her. Of course, it had drawn her right into trouble. But as she considered Jared's chiseled profile, expressive eyes, and the intentness with which he guarded Evelyn Granger, she realized that if she had to be in a jam, Jared Slater was exactly the man she wanted looking out for her.

She fidgeted in her seat, uncomfortable with the tack her thoughts had taken. "I'd never make it as a detective. All this inactivity is driving me bananas."

"We have no choice. She didn't take my warning seriously." He passed her a paper bag filled with Twinkies and bottled fruit juice he'd purchased that afternoon. "Sorry about the limited dinner menu."

"What good will sitting here do?" She played along with his delusion, hoping to persuade him to give it up.

"If someone wants to kill Mrs. Granger, she lives alone. Why wouldn't the killer just wait until she's asleep and break in?"

"That's not his M.O."

"M.O.?"

"Modus operandi," Jared had explained. "Each of the other victims was shot late at night in a secluded area away from their homes. He must have followed them for days, learning their routines, watching for the right opportunity."

She leaned against the headrest and closed her eyes. If Jared had to dream, why couldn't he concoct nice, normal male fantasies, like being chased by naked, big-breasted women on a desert island?

Sometime later the punch of an elbow in her rib cage had awakened her. "She's walking the dog."

"Now that's the most excitement we've had in hours," she grumbled sarcastically. "How long do we keep this up?"

"Until we catch some sign of the killer. Once he's arrested, Evelyn Granger will be safe." He twisted in the seat to keep an eye on Mrs. Granger, who had paused on the other side of the street while the Pekingese watered a neighbor's mailbox.

Tyler bit her lip in frustration. Even if there *was* a killer, Jared wouldn't know him if the man walked up and kicked him. For the hundredth time, she'd wondered how anyone could possess such a frustrating mix of normalcy and insanity.

To avoid saying something she would regret, she'd scrunched down in her seat and kept quiet.

They'd waited for an hour after Mrs. Granger's lights had gone out at midnight. Jared had finally admitted the woman was probably safe for the remainder of the night and they could return to the Residence Inn and grab some sleep.

Now, Tyler snuggled gratefully into the fresh sheets of the bed, stretched to turn off the beside light, then drifted into unconsciousness.

THE TRILL OF A mockingbird outside her window awakened her, and sunlight flooded the room. She stretched lazily, grateful Jared hadn't awakened her with predawn nightmares.

After a quick shower, she dressed in shorts, a cotton T-shirt, and sandals, then sauntered downstairs. The Murphy bed was folded back into the wall and the sound of the shower in the downstairs bathroom informed her that Jared was awake.

She switched on the television in the sitting area and listened to the local news as she filled the coffee maker.

As the announcer read the latest headline, her hand froze at the faucet. "Around one-fifteen this morning as she walked her dog, Evelyn Witek Granger, longtime Micanopy resident and antique dealer, was shot to death."

Tyler dropped the carafe with a crash, and glass splintered in the stainless-steel sink.

Jared Slater wasn't crazy, after all.

Chapter Eight

"Leave it," Jared spoke behind her. "The house-keeping staff can clean up the glass after we're gone."

Slack-jawed with amazement, Tyler abandoned the shattered coffee carafe and turned to face him. Evelyn Granger was dead, just as Jared had predicted, and *he* couldn't have done it. They were driving back to their motel at the time Evelyn's killer had struck. "Your dreams were right—"

Everything made sense now. Jared wasn't the paradox of mania and reason she'd found so hard to comprehend. The torment in his eyes wasn't madness, but misery flowing from some paranormal wellspring that provided him a glimpse of future tragedies—tragedies he'd so far been unable to forestall. Water dripped from his hair, running down his high cheekbones like tears, but the agony in his eyes mirrored suffering too deep for weeping.

What a fool she'd been. She should have known he wasn't crazy. Then again, perhaps some part of her *had* sensed the truth. Maybe that was why she'd stayed with him, and now yearned to comfort him, to wrap her arms around him and beg forgiveness for having doubted him.

She moved toward him, then halted at the sound of the continuing newscast.

"Police," the announcer droned in a bland Midwestern accent, "are looking for this man and his female companion for questioning."

Tyler stumbled into the sitting area and listened in horror as the newscaster dictated a detailed description of her, Jared, and their rental car.

"What are we going to do?" she asked. "They probably want to talk to us because we came into town asking about her. But we can't tell them the truth. They'll never believe it."

Jared, barefoot and dressed only in jeans, pulled her into his arms and clasped her shivering body against the warm expanse of his muscled chest. His lips moved against her hair, and his breath warmed her cheek. "You didn't believe me until now, did you?"

She tilted her head and met his gaze. "Can you blame me?"

He tightened his arms around her. "If you thought I was crazy, why did you stay?"

Heat flamed her face. She wanted to admit she was falling in love with him, but the words lodged in her throat.

"It must have been the hazardous-duty pay," he said. He released her and stepped away, avoiding her eyes. "And the duty just became more hazardous."

"With the police after us?"

He turned and met her gaze head-on. "That, too."

"Too?" Fear cinched her lungs, squeezing out the air. "What else is there?"

"I'm giving you a month's severance pay and a plane ticket to Raleigh-Durham," he said. "I'll pay someone to drive your car back to Chapel Hill, too."

"Whoa." She held up her hands in objection. "We've been down this road before. I didn't say I wanted to quit."

He crossed his arms over his chest in a stance that defied protest. "You don't have a choice. I'm firing you."

Anger and hurt flooded through her. "Why? The killer's still out there. Don't you want my help in finding him?"

"There's no time to argue." His granite expression didn't waver. "The police will figure out where we are soon, so we have to get moving. I'll drop you at the nearest airport."

"I've been shot at, almost killed in a car crash, and the police are after me, all because of you." Her voice swelled in pitch and volume. "And now you're booting me out without an explanation? You owe me better than that."

His stony look melted, to be replaced by an expression of such tenderness and pain, it took her breath away. He placed his arm around her and drew her down on the love seat beside him. Cradling her cheeks in his hands, he probed her face with pain-filled eyes.

"My greatest hope was to avert Evelyn Granger's death—and to prove to you that the murders in my dreams are not inevitable."

She covered his hands with hers. "It's not your fault. How were you to know Evelyn Granger would walk her dog again in the wee hours of the morning?"

"The killer knew." He dropped his hands to her shoulders. "Don't you see? I have to find this man before he kills again."

"All the more reason for me to stay and help," she said, tracing his cheekbone with her finger.

He grasped her hand and pressed his lips against her palm, creating a pleasurable surge of warmth through her. Abruptly, he dropped her hand, stood and moved away. "You *can't* stay."

His rejection stung, but she couldn't leave him, not now. "I won't—"

"You have no choice." He whipped around to confront her, brown eyes blazing with flecks of green fire. "*You* are his next victim."

Shock robbed her of breath. "You've dreamed about *me?*"

He nodded, and the gravity of his expression frightened her as much as his revelation. "Before I ever met you."

His initial reluctance to hire her, his blunt attempts to send her away when the storm eased made sense now. He'd been *protecting* her. Dear God, if she'd been halfway in love with him before, he had just

pushed her over the precipice, and there was no turning back. "I can't leave you to face this alone."

Stubbornness flashed across his taut features. "And
I can't allow you to stay and be killed."

She crossed the room, twined her arms around his
chest, and pressed her cheek against his heart. He remained as rigid and unresponsive as a fence post.

"Your dreams don't always have to come true," she
said. "If we'd waited just a few minutes longer at Mrs.
Granger's, we could have scared the killer away."

He clutched her to him with a fury that drove the air
from her lungs. "Don't you see? If I know what the
killer is thinking, it's possible he knows my thoughts,
as well. Maybe he knew we were there and simply
waited until we left."

She splayed her fingers across the firm flesh of his
chest; keeping contact with his reassuring heat drove
away her terror. "Are you sure he can read your
thoughts?"

He pulled her close again and rested his chin on her
hair. "No, but it seems a reasonable explanation. The
killer's always one step ahead of me, and I can never
catch up."

She swallowed hard and forced herself to pose a
question whose answer she dreaded. "What did you
dream about me—about my death?"

Only the droning voice of the TV weatherman reverberated in the room, and seconds ticked away before Jared answered. "It happens at my house at Lake
Toxaway."

She sensed he was holding back, but she didn't press him for details. What he'd revealed gave her the opening she needed. "Then, as long as I don't return to the mountain house with you, I'm safe?"

He nodded. "So far, the actual murders haven't varied from what I've dreamed."

"Then I'd better pack, so we can get out of here before the police come looking for us."

She felt the tension ease from his muscles before he released her. "Then you agree to go home to Chapel Hill?"

No way. Jared feared she would be killed if she stayed with him, but only Jared knew the killer's mind. Therefore, only Jared could keep her safe. Besides, who else would protect her? Certainly not Gran.

She had to stay with Jared. Even if she wasn't falling in love with him, she couldn't leave him now. She needed him to keep her alive.

"I agree to stay away from Lake Toxaway. But you're not getting rid of me." She rose on tiptoe and brushed his lips with a fleeting kiss, then raced up the stairs before he could respond.

GRIPPING HIS LUGGAGE, Jared sprinted across the four-lane road that ran beneath the interstate.

Tyler, carrying her bags, kept pace beside him. "Where are we going?"

In the May sun, reflecting with August intensity off the pavement, Jared crossed the parking lot of the motel diagonally across from the Residence Inn.

"Room 107. I called for a cab to meet us there in fifteen minutes."

"But our rental car—"

"If the police have our descriptions, you can bet they have that license number by now, too."

He held open the lobby door, then followed her inside. The air-conditioned air hit him like an arctic blast, and a desk clerk glanced up at their approach. "May I help you?"

"Do you have a gift shop?" Jared kept his voice casual. Their escape depended on not drawing undue attention.

The clerk pointed down a hallway, and Jared motioned Tyler ahead. Halfway down the hall, he followed her into a cubbyhole of a shop, stuffed with Florida tourist souvenirs, postcards, T-shirts, and flamingo yard ornaments in Day-Glo pink.

Tyler picked up a cigarette lighter shaped like an orange and replaced it with a shudder of disgust. "What are we doing here?"

"Camouflage." Jared snatched a pair of Ray•Ban sunglasses and a University of Florida Gators ball cap from the racks.

Copying his example, Tyler selected red-framed sunglasses with huge lenses and a wide-brimmed straw hat with an attached scarf to cover her dark hair. He paid for their purchases in cash.

"Where's the closest Nations Bank?" he asked the clerk as she bagged their items.

She rattled off an address that he committed to memory.

When they stepped out of the shop, he directed Tyler toward a rear entrance that led to the pool. Still carrying their luggage, they skirted the landscaped pool deck and ducked through a passageway filled with maids' carts and a vibrating ice machine, which gave access to the parking lot in front of rooms 101-123. He stopped in front of Room 107 and piled their bags by the curb.

While they waited for the cab, he removed their purchases from the bag and ripped off the tags. After donning the sunglasses, he pulled the bill of the cap low over his eyes.

Tyler adjusted her sunglasses, then tucked her French braid beneath the crown of the straw hat and tied the scarf at her nape to cover the rest of her hair.

"All I need is a second-degree sunburn to look like a genuine tourist," she said with a wry grin.

His heart wrenched at the sight of her, smiling up at him behind huge goggle lenses. She hadn't abandoned him, even when she'd believed he was crazy. Now, with the threat of death hanging over her, her courage hadn't wavered. Her continued refusal to desert him touched his lonely heart. He silently vowed to protect her, with his life if necessary. The danger she faced made him more determined than ever to catch the unrelenting killer who stalked his dreams.

"Here's the cab." She pointed to a vehicle rounding the corner of the motel.

Jared breathed a silent prayer of thanks. So far, so good,

A few minutes later, the cab deposited them in front of a suburban branch bank, and Jared removed their bags and stacked them by a street bench.

"I won't be long," he told her. "Try not to look too conspicuous."

He endeavored to follow his own advice as he entered the bank lobby and extracted his bankcard from his wallet, but remaining inconspicuous would be tough once he requested $20,000 in cash. Within hours, he wouldn't be able to access his account without fear of being traced. Twenty thousand would have to suffice until they'd located the killer.

The fresh-faced young teller seemed unimpressed with the size of his withdrawal and counted out his cash with a polite but bored expression. Jared forced himself to saunter from the bank, knowing it was just a matter of time before the police connected with Bobbie Hendrix and learned his identity.

He cursed himself for a fool when he saw Tyler sitting on the green bench, her head back against the seat as if basking in the sun. She looked like a very attractive tourist in her sunhat and red-and-white sundress. If he'd kicked her out when she'd first arrived on the mountain, she would be safe now. Instead, in his selfishness, he'd kept her close. Now, somehow, he had to convince her that her trust in him made her more vulnerable, not safer.

She didn't move as he approached, giving the impression of someone without a care or any need to hurry. He strolled past her to a pay phone, checked the Yellow Pages, and called another cab.

Thirty long minutes later, the cabbie unloaded them and their luggage in front of Fast Eddie's Used Cars, a dilapidated building on an unpaved lot on the town's northeast side. A seedy salesman in a rumpled seersucker suit and white patent-leather shoes raised a cloud of dust in his haste to meet them.

"Welcome to Fast Eddie's, folks," he greeted them in an oily tone. "Home of the best used cars in the state."

"I need a car guaranteed to take us as far as Jacksonville," Jared said.

"Jacksonville?" the salesman sputtered in mock outrage. "Any one of these fine automobiles will take you across the country and back again without a problem, Mr.—?"

"Simpson, Bart Simpson," Jared replied with a straight face.

The salesman didn't blink. "What price range do you have in mind, Bart?"

"Fifteen hundred."

"That's too expensive," Tyler murmured beside him, playing along as they'd planned in the cab, knowing they would draw suspicion if they seemed too eager.

"But I—" Jared began.

"We can't afford that much. You see—" she turned her charm on the salesman "—we were on our way back from Disney World when someone ran us off the interstate and totaled our car. Bart has an important business appointment tomorrow morning in Jacksonville, so we have to hurry home."

"Now, dear—" Jared objected, warming to his henpecked-husband role.

"But with our vacation expenses," Tyler went on, "we just can't afford more than a thousand."

"Sweetheart, why don't we just rent a car like I wanted to in the first place?" Jared suggested in a timid tone.

"Because that's throwing away money," she insisted in a whine. "If we buy a cheap car, we can get our money back by reselling it. You'll never see rental fees again."

"You're so right, Mrs. Simpson," the salesman crooned. "I have just the car for you. Follow me."

Jared signaled Tyler to precede him, and they picked their way between rows of cars better suited for a junkyard than for sale. The salesman halted in front of a 1972 Plymouth Fury with faded green paint, rust spots, and a flaking vinyl roof. Large numerals across the windshield proclaimed a price of $1200.

"Oh, my, that's too much," Tyler protested in her Mrs. Simpson voice.

"For you, nine hundred."

"Seven hundred cash," Jared countered.

The salesman delayed all of one second. "Sold."

LESS THAN AN HOUR LATER, Jared approached Interstate 75 and turned south toward Tampa. Behind him, the Plymouth laid a trail of oily smoke.

"We'll be lucky if this piece of junk makes it as far as Tampa," he grumbled.

"Tampa? But that's the wrong direction," Tyler shouted over the rush of hot air through the open windows. The air-conditioning had failed two blocks from the lot.

"We'll be less conspicuous at a large airport like TIA." He kept an eye on the rearview mirror, alert for signs of the highway patrol, and prayed that Fast Eddie, if questioned, would point the authorities toward Jacksonville.

"Where do we go from Tampa?" she asked.

"Wherever we can find Detective Sam Witek, if he's still alive."

"Who's Sam Witek?"

He eased off the gas. The last thing they needed was to be stopped for speeding. "Witek was Pete Stanwick's partner on the Ozzie Anderson case, remember?"

"Why are we looking for him? You ruled out a connection between him and Stanwick and Molinsky."

"Didn't you hear the announcer this morning? Evelyn Granger's maiden name was Witek. That connects her to Mary Stanwick and Veronica Molinsky. Maybe Sam Witek can tell us how."

TYLER RECLINED AGAINST the plush seat of the limousine as it sped out of the Boston airport and breathed in the scent of fine leather and the faintest hint of cigar smoke. "Why go to all this expense when you can rent a car?"

"The same reason we didn't rent a car in Gainesville. We'd have to show identification, and even this far north, it could lead the authorities to us. With a limo, all we need is cash." Jared patted his bag on the seat beside him.

She studied him from behind her sunglasses. During the drive to Tampa and the flight to Boston, he may have appeared relaxed to the casual observer, but the twitch in the tiny muscle at the base of his jaw proved otherwise. As the limo cleared the outskirts of the city and headed into the country, his tension eased.

She inspected the fully-stocked bar, television, car phone and fax machine, and the glass panel that separated them from Enrico, the bull-necked, uniformed driver. "At this rate, you'll run through Grandfather Slater's trust fund in a week."

At her words, the muscle in his jaw flexed again. "This shouldn't take that long."

He draped an arm around her shoulders and she snuggled into his embrace. Once they'd boarded the plane, they had avoided discussing their plans for fear of being overheard in the crowded cabin, but now she needed to know his strategy.

"How do you expect to find Sam Witek?" she asked.

His lips moved against her hair. "Police partners usually develop strong bonds. I'll simply ask Pete Stanwick if he has kept up with his old partner over the years."

Only the sanctuary of Jared's embrace seemed real to Tyler. Her mind whirled as she tried to make sense of the rest. They were speeding along winding Massachusetts byways in a luxurious limo in pursuit of a killer Jared knew only from his dreams. Facing the comparative inactivity of research would be a challenge after these adventures—if she survived. A tremor shook her at the thought of Jared's faceless killer stalking her.

"You okay?" His mellow baritone sounded in her ear.

"No," she replied with more honesty than she'd intended.

He tilted her chin until their eyes met. "Then let me send you home where it's safe."

She stared into the depths of eyes as brown as dark chocolate. "The only place I feel safe is with you."

With a strangled cry, he brought his mouth down and claimed hers.

She twined her arms around his neck and returned the sweet pressure of his lips, thankful she was sitting down as her knees weakened. The heat of his body seared the length of her, and his fingers tangled in her hair, drawing her closer as he consumed her with his fiery kiss. Passion exorcised her reason as she yielded to desire, forgetting everything but the man whose heart hammered against her breasts.

He drew back, his hands clasping her shoulders, and stared at her with a face contorted in agony. "You're not safe, Tyler, especially not with me."

"Then we'll just have to catch this killer, won't we?" she answered with a gravity that matched his.

He pulled her to him again, tucked her head beneath his chin, and they rode in silence through the afternoon shadows falling upon the rolling countryside and tiny farm villages.

The shadows had lengthened into dusk when the limo pulled to the curb in front of a neat brick bungalow. In the dim light, Tyler noted the bedraggled state of the flower beds that edged the walk. The gardening must have been Mary Stanwick's responsibility.

While Enrico waited, she and Jared walked to the door and rang the bell. Lightless windows and dead quiet convinced her the house was empty. The jangle of the doorbell could be heard echoing throughout the house.

"Maybe Pete moved after Mary died," she suggested.

"It's possible." Jared surveyed the nearby houses. "Maybe a neighbor could tell us."

He had stepped off the porch when the front door opened. A young man, dressed in jeans and a Harvard sweatshirt, appraised them with bleary eyes.

"Mr. Stanwick, I'm Jared Slater and this is Tyler Harris."

She nodded at the man who was too young to be Pete Stanwick. He had to be his son.

"What do you want?" he asked.

"I'm a reporter," Jared explained, "looking into the murder of your mother. May I speak with your father?"

Stanwick stared past them to the street. "Since when do reporters arrive in limousines?"

Jared placed an arm around Tyler's shoulders and hugged her. "When they're forced by a cruel editor to combine an assignment with their honeymoon. Is your father in?"

"He's at his fishing cabin in New Hampshire. I don't know when he'll be back."

Picking up the lead from Jared, Tyler flashed Stanwick a smile. "Then maybe you could help us. The sooner my husband finishes this story, the sooner we can leave on our wedding trip."

The young man raked long fingers through his tousled hair. "I'm studying for exams—"

"I promise," Jared said, "this won't take long."

"Okay," Stanwick agreed. "Shoot."

Tyler winced at his unfortunate choice of words.

Jared tugged a notebook from the pocket of his jeans, flipped it open, and pulled a pen from his shirt pocket. "Have the local authorities come up with any leads on your mother's killer?"

Young Stanwick's face clouded. "Yeah, they've tried to blame it on my father."

Tyler bit back an exclamation of surprise and left the comments to Jared. He was supposed to be the reporter, she the lovestruck bride.

"Your father?" Jared asked in a shocked tone. "Why blame him?"

"They discovered he and Mom had been arguing over Dad's drinking for weeks before Mom died. They put that together with the fact she'd been killed by a .357, the same caliber as Dad's service revolver."

Jared scribbled some hasty notes. "Were the bullets a match?"

Stanwick shook his head. "The bullet that killed Mom was too distorted to match anything. Needless to say, the suspicions of his fellow officers hit Dad pretty hard. That's why he spends so much time at his cabin. It's the only place not filled with memories of Mom."

Tyler strained to catch Jared's reaction, but the twilight shadows obscured his face.

Jared flipped another page in his notebook. "Did your father keep in touch with Sam Witek, his former partner?"

"Uncle Sammie? Yeah, they've always been close." Stanwick squinted at them in the darkness. "What's Uncle Sammie got to do with this?"

"Maybe nothing," Jared assured him. "We'd just like to talk with him."

Stanwick flicked on the porch light. "Too late."

Tyler's hopes plummeted, and she forgot her declaration to keep silent. "He's dead?"

Stanwick shrugged. "As close to it as you can get and still be breathing. He's at the Roseland Nursing Home, on the west side of town on the main highway. They'll be putting him to bed about now."

"Thanks for your time." Jared pocketed his notebook.

Tyler took his arm as he started down the walkway.

"Mr. Slater," Stanwick called after them.

Jared paused and looked back. "Yeah?"

Silhouetted by the porch light, Stanwick stood on the top step, his hands in his pockets. "If you find the bastard that killed my mother, I'd like to know. I have a score to settle with him."

ILLUMINATED STARKLY by the naked bulb of a goose-necked lamp, a grimace twisted the stranger's lips as he adjusted the tiny wires of a contraption on the scarred desktop.

"You're in for a big surprise, Jared Slater," he muttered to himself. "The last one you'll ever get."

Perspiration beaded his forehead and ran into his eyes as he completed the last step of his creation. He exerted all his willpower to keep his gloved hands from trembling. One false move and he would blow himself and everyone in the adjoining rooms to kingdom come.

After completing the final adjustment, he slid the carefully constructed apparatus into a priority envelope bearing Slater's Lake Toxaway address. He secured the trip wire to the zippered opening, gingerly sealed the flap and affixed the stamps. He would deliver it to the post office tomorrow morning.

He sat back with a whoosh of relief, wiped his brow, and tried to relax his hands. They shook as if he were coming off a three-day drunk. He rose on unsteady legs, flexed the kinks from his cramped muscles, and poured a double whiskey into a smudged glass. He drank greedily before reclining on the sagging mattress of the hotel bed.

Things had a way of working out. He'd lost Slater and the woman after the screw-up on the interstate. He'd been delirious with fever, and if he hadn't blacked out at the rest area, he could have finished off Slater's girlfriend then.

When he'd awakened to find them leaving, he'd pursued, intending to shoot the girl as he passed their Volvo on the highway. But when he'd pulled even with them, dizziness had almost caused him to lose consciousness. Twice he'd lost control of his car, crashing it into theirs. In his rearview mirror, he'd watched the Volvo flip and roll before he took off for the next exit.

He'd ditched the Blazer and holed up in a fleabag motel until the next morning. By the time he'd discovered that Slater and his girl had survived the crash, their trail was cold.

No matter. The delay had created only a small blip in his timetable. No Rest For The Wicked.

His satisfied chuckle split the silence. It didn't matter where Slater was. He had to go home sometime, and when he did, he'd have a booming reception waiting for him.

Chapter Nine

For the first time since he'd awakened that morning
and learned Evelyn Granger had been killed, Jared
allowed himself to relax.

The fire's soft glow and twinkling candles on the
tables provided the only light in the almost-deserted
dining room of the Birch and Bottle Inn. Dark beams
traversed the ceiling above timber-framed walls and
formed the rough-hewn mantel above the huge fireplace. Pewter mugs and platters glimmered on the
plate rails, and the floor sloped as it neared the base of
the massive chimney, where it had settled over centu-
ries.

At the far end of the room, past the bar, laughter
sounded as Enrico and the innkeeper competed in a
game of darts. Across the table, Tyler was dressed in
her red sweater and jeans that would keep out the New
England spring chill. Her eyes sparkled in the candlelight as she sipped coffee.

He thought enviously of that other Jared Slater in
an alternate universe, secluded in a quaint country inn

with the woman of his dreams. *Dreams.* He silently cursed the word. His dreams caused nothing but misery. True, a dream had provided his first glimpse of Tyler, but it had also forecast her death. In that alternate universe, another carefree Jared would probably make love to her and propose marriage about now. But not in this world. Maybe not in this lifetime—unless he found the killer who threatened the woman he loved.

The woman he loved. The words jolted him from his daydreams as he acknowledged his feelings for the woman across the table. But he couldn't tell her—not now, not until he was convinced she was safe.

"That was a magnificent meal." She patted her lips with a damask napkin and leaned back with a smile of satisfaction. "Enrico knew what he was talking about when he recommended this place."

Jared nodded toward the dart players. "Looks like our driver comes here often."

Her gaze stole around the cozy room. "I don't know how they stay in business with so few guests."

"It's early yet. The summer season doesn't begin until after Memorial Day." He gauged her troubled expression but doubted her concern for the inn's profit-making. "What's on your mind?"

She fidgeted with her napkin and avoided his eyes. "Nothing."

"Don't play games with me, Tyler. There's too much at stake."

"Sorry." Even in the dim light, her blush was evident. "I've just been wondering why you identified yourself to Stanwick's son, but when you registered here, you used a fake name and pretended we were married."

"Stanwick has met me before, so I couldn't risk making him suspicious by using another name," he explained. "But Enrico thinks we're Mr. and Mrs. Simpson, a honeymooning couple avoiding friends and family. If the Florida authorities have issued a national alert for us, I want to make it as difficult as possible for them to track us."

He tore his attention from the hypnotizing honesty of her huge gray eyes. He hadn't exactly lied, but there was no need to remind her a cold-blooded killer was searching for them, as well. The clerk at the registration desk had assured him their room had a sitting area. He would sleep on the sofa with his gun beneath his pillow, just in case his dreams weren't as infallible as they seemed. If Tyler suffered so much as a scratch, he could never live with himself.

When they entered the cozy room with its blazing fire, canopied bed, and heavy curtains closed against the darkness outside, his resolve to keep his distance almost melted. He longed to draw her to him, wrap her in his embrace and hold her throughout the night. He squelched his desire with memories of the killer who stalked his dreams.

Losing control and kissing her in the limo had been a mistake. It was only one kiss, but the taste of her had created a hunger a lifetime of kisses couldn't satisfy. If he kissed her again, he could never send her away.

But he had to keep his distance, so that when the time came, she would leave willingly, without regret. So that he would have the strength to make her go. Otherwise, her blood would be on his hands.

"We have a big day tomorrow. We'd better get some sleep." His words came out more brusquely than he'd intended, and his heart wrenched at her bewildered expression.

He lifted a blanket from the foot of the bed, took one of its pillows and pitched them onto the sofa before removing the pistol from his suitcase. He tucked it beneath the pillow and sat to remove his shoes.

She stared at the sofa where he'd concealed the gun. "You brought that on the plane?"

"It was in my luggage."

"Isn't that illegal?"

"Not if I declared the gun and my luggage was locked." No need to tell her he hadn't declared it. He had feared drawing attention that would cause the ticket clerk to remember them if questioned.

She crossed the room and placed her hand on his shoulder. "You don't have to sleep on the sofa."

He issued up a silent prayer for strength and removed her hand. If he made love to her now, sending her away to safety later would be too hard. "We can't let anything distract us. If we lower our guard for one minute, we might give the killer the opportunity he needs."

Besides, if he yielded to his yearning, he would never get her out of his mind—and a killer might know his thoughts. The more he could focus on something besides Tyler, the better.

Hurt joined bewilderment in her eyes. "I thought you agreed I was safe, away from your mountain."

He hardened his heart against her. "Assumptions, like desire, could get you killed."

JARED AWOKE WITH a soreness in his neck and a disposition to match. Sleep had been almost impossible with temptation only a few feet away. He'd spent restless hours during the night, watching the gentle rise and fall of her breasts, the seductive curve of her hip beneath the covers, the flutter of thick eyelashes against her rosy cheeks as she dreamed. Hell, even his murderous nightmares would have been less torturous than battling his longing for her.

With relief that the agonizing night had finally ended, he tossed back the blanket, gathered fresh clothes from his suitcase, and went into the bathroom to shower.

Twenty minutes later, dressed and shaved, he entered the bedroom to find Tyler sitting cross-legged in the middle of the bed in front of a huge breakfast tray. She had donned a crimson velour robe and brushed her hair, which lay like an ebony cloud on her shoulders.

She poured aromatic coffee from a silver pot and handed him a cup. "There's orange juice, too, cranberry muffins, and this morning's Boston *Globe*."

"Anything in it about us?" He carried his coffee to the sofa.

"Nothing. Guess we're small potatoes in the big scheme of things." She grinned, broke off a piece of muffin, and popped it into her mouth. "Want some?"

He was starving, but not for food. He diverted his eyes to the morning's headlines. "We'll head for Roseland Nursing Home right after breakfast."

She shook her head. "I called while you were in the shower. Visiting hours don't begin until afternoon. What do you suggest we do in the meantime?"

He groaned inwardly, knowing all too well how he would like to spend the morning. He surveyed the rumpled covers of the wide bed, but he clamped a lid on his longing and steered his thoughts to the killer. "We can investigate the allegations that Pete Stanwick killed his wife."

She paused with a piece of muffin halfway to her lips. "Do you think he did?"

He shrugged. "He may have had reason to kill his wife, but Veronica Molinsky and Evelyn Granger? According to my dreams, they were all killed by the same man, and Stanwick doesn't appear to have a motive."

She dusted crumbs from her hands and climbed off the bed. "Maybe the local police can tell us something."

"Yeah—" he couldn't keep the sarcasm from his tone "—maybe the local police can lock us up for extradition to Florida."

Undeterred, Tyler approached, leaned forward and planted a feathery kiss on his forehead. "Then it's a good thing you brought along your researcher. A town this size has to have a local paper and a library."

He used every ounce of willpower to restrain himself, but if his lack of response bothered her, she didn't show it. After gathering her clothes, she disappeared into the bathroom, leaving him alone to wrestle with his conscience and his heart.

DUST MOTES DANCED in the sunlight streaming through the Palladian windows of the library reference room. Tyler flipped through bound back issues of the *Village Crier,* searching for articles on Mary Stanwick's murder. Across the room, Jared sat at a microfiche viewer, reading old stories of Ozzie Anderson's crimes.

At the turn of a page, a headline jumped out at her: Detective Resigns in Wake of Wife's Murder. The grainy photograph was indecipherable, especially with Stanwick's uniform cap pulled low over his eyes. Reading quickly, she scribbled additions to her notes.

An hour later, stiff-necked, with her nostrils itching from dust, Tyler closed the volume and returned it to its cubbyhole in the periodicals section. At the same time, Jared completed his notes from the microfiche and shoved himself to his feet. The legs of his chair screeched in the unnatural silence.

"Shh," the librarian hissed. She was a little prune of a woman with white hair, safe behind the fortress of the massive oak circulation desk.

Jared threw an apologetic smile at the tiny tyrant, took Tyler's elbow, and led her quickly out into the cool spring air, heavy with the fragrance of lilacs.

"Do they teach that in library school?" He steered her toward a bench in the town square beneath the statue of a local patriot in the Revolutionary War.

"How to take notes?" she asked.

"Uh-uh. That withering stare and shushing noise that turns strong men's blood to ice water and their knees to mush."

She smiled, glad to see his sense of humor had returned. His uncharacteristic surliness at breakfast had bewildered her, until she'd realized he probably hadn't slept well on the sofa. Now, however, an engaging smile lifted a corner of his mouth and his eyes twinkled.

"You must have found something useful," she suggested.

He expelled an enormous sigh and extracted his notebook from his pocket. "Nothing that points to our killer. There's a touching story from four years ago about Ozzie Anderson's son's frantic last-ditch efforts to save his father from execution. Arnie was only six years old when his father was arrested, and he spent most of his adult years trying to free his old man.''

''Does that make Arnie a suspect?''

''Maybe. The papers listed his address, so we'll check him out before we visit Witek. What did you find?''

She unfolded her notes. ''Pretty much what Stanwick's son told us. Circumstantial evidence points to Pete in Mary's death—a history of quarrels, a weapon similar to Pete's, Pete's lack of an alibi at the time of the killing. But the district attorney refused to press charges, claiming they wouldn't stick in court.''

''Was Pete fired from the department?''

She could almost see the wheels turning behind his intense hazel eyes. ''Not exactly. 'Encouraged to resign' is the phrase the paper used.''

Jared stretched and rubbed the back of his neck. ''Which brings us back to where we started. Maybe Sam Witek can shed some light on all this. But first, we'll pay Arnie Anderson a visit. The family farm is just outside town.''

In the cushy confines of the limo, Tyler giggled. ''Enrico is going to wonder what kind of honeymoon we're on.''

Jared smiled, making her wish the honeymoon was real. ''At what I'm paying him, he could drive us in circles and not ask questions.''

She gazed out through a cloud of dust. ''This road isn't even paved.''

"We'll tell him we're hunting antiques. As I remember, you're something of an expert."

She remembered the Roseville vase, stuffed among the clothes in her suitcase, and the kind woman, now dead, who had sold it to her. She shivered in the climate-controlled atmosphere.

The car slowed and stopped in front of a run-down farmhouse. Gangly bushes of lavender lilacs bloomed on either side of the front steps, the only spots of color against the weathered boards of the ancient two-story structure. The farmhouse had been battered by the elements until no trace of paint remained. A screen door sagged on its hinges, its bottom panel torn and ragged. Verdant lilac leaves provided the only green in the dirt yard, populated by a few scraggly hens and an aged rooster.

The screen door banged, and a heavy woman in a shapeless cotton dress, both as colorless as the house, took a stance on the top step with her pudgy hands on her hips. As they approached, she tugged an old sweater across her ample bosom.

"Mrs. Anderson?" Jared asked.

She nodded, and her double chin trembled. "If you folks are from that damn publisher, I done told him I want no part of no book. Ozzie's dead and gone, and I got peace for the first time in my life. Leave him buried."

"We're not from any publisher, Mrs. Anderson," Jared assured her.

The fat woman eyed the limousine with suspicion. "Then what do you want with me?"

"Actually," Tyler replied, "we're looking for your son."

Comprehension lighted Mrs. Anderson's squinting eyes. "Collection agency, eh? You folks must do all right to drive such a fancy rig."

"We're not from a collection agency," Jared said. "I'm doing research on capital punishment, and I'd like to talk with Arnie about his experience with the appeals board."

Her skeptical expression deepened. "Well, if you find him, you let me know. He took off for Alaska, looking for work, right after his daddy died. I ain't seen or heard from him since."

She turned on her heel with remarkable quickness for a woman her size and disappeared into the decaying farmhouse, slamming the screen door behind her.

Jared grimaced. "That was a colossal waste of time."

Tyler considered the depressing farmhouse. "Just think of it as sight-seeing."

AFTER LUNCH AT A LOCAL mom-and-pop restaurant that served thick, juicy hamburgers with all the trimmings, Jared directed Enrico to drive across town to Roseland Nursing Home.

The low brick structure with barred windows and bedraggled lawns squelched Tyler's feeling of well-being. The bed of sickly rosebushes that gave the place its name did nothing to ease the bleak atmosphere.

"Looks more like a penal colony than a rest home," she observed.

Jared's expression of distaste indicated he shared her opinion. "The sooner we're out of here, the better."

The atmosphere deteriorated further when they stepped through the front doors. The bare green walls and yellowed linoleum seemed clean enough, but the overpowering stench of disinfectant assaulted Tyler's nostrils.

"We're here to see Sam Witek," Jared announced to a burly male attendant behind the reception desk.

The orderly shoved a clipboard toward them with a sign-in sheet, and Jared wrote Mr. and Mrs. B. Simpson. Tyler suppressed a smile and whispered in his ear, "If you tire of Simpson, we can always resort to Beavis and Butthead."

Her smile faded as they headed down a corridor toward Room 122. Patients hailed them, some calling them by unfamiliar names.

With relief, she followed Jared into Sam Witek's room, wondering if the man's reason had degenerated with his body, but alert black eyes in a withered face confronted them from his pillow.

Jared introduced himself and Tyler, and Witek waved with a feeble gesture toward chairs beside the bed.

"It's good to have visitors," he wheezed. "Most folks avoid this place. What can I do for you?"

"I'm sorry about your sister Evelyn," Tyler said.

Tears filled Witek's eyes. "My kid sister... and me so wasted, I can't even attend her funeral."

"We're looking for Evelyn's killer," Jared said, "and we're hoping you can help us."

"Me?" Witek's question dissolved into a racking cough. "I'm not much help to anyone these days."

Tyler placed her hand over Witek's. "You've done some great detective work in your day, Mr. Witek. We could use your expertise."

While Jared filled Witek in on the three murdered women, Tyler surveyed the room. A green oxygen tank sat close to the bed with a mask dangling from its regulator. Between that and Witek's labored breathing, she guessed he suffered from some type of respiratory illness. On the wall above his bed hung a silver crucifix, and framed family pictures, including a smiling photograph of Evelyn Granger. A few mystery novels and a thick picture album filled a shelf below the window.

"These three women are connected somehow," Jared concluded. "If you help us determine how, maybe we can find this man before he kills again."

Witek lay pale against his pillow. "Ozzie Anderson," he said. "His case was the only one of Pete's and mine that Larry Molinsky prosecuted. Ozzie has to be the connection."

"But Ozzie's dead," she said.

Witek reached for the oxygen mask and inhaled deeply. "You don't know these men like I do, miss. Once they're locked away with no hope of reprieve, they're consumed by the desire for revenge."

Jared nodded. "Wanting revenge is understandable, but attaining it *after* they're dead—"

"They make friends in the Big House," Witek said, "with guys whose souls are as twisted as their own."

"Are you suggesting Anderson convinced another inmate to carry out his revenge killing for him?" she asked.

Breathless, Witek nodded. "It's possible."

Tyler shook her head. "But why would the killer go after your sister and not you?"

Witek mustered an ironic smile. "Killing me wouldn't be revenge, it would be a favor."

After bidding Witek goodbye, they returned to the limo and Jared instructed Enrico to drive back to the Birch and Bottle.

"Now we're making progress." Jared slipped her arm through his and pulled her closer. "Witek may be on to something. Maybe Anderson persuaded a friend to kill for him."

Tyler laid her head on Jared's shoulder, but even his comforting presence couldn't stanch her questions. "How do we find out who Anderson's friends were? Mrs. Anderson's already refused to talk to us."

Jared's eyes glinted with excitement. "We ask the warden."

"YOU HAVE A CALL, Mr. Simpson." The innkeeper pointed to a telephone alcove in the hallway outside the dining room. "You can take it there if you wish."

Tyler accepted another cup of after-dinner coffee from the waitress and sat back to wait. When they'd returned to the inn, Jared had placed a call to the warden of the New Jersey State Penitentiary, and as the hour grew late, they'd both feared he wouldn't return the call until the next day. The postponement gnawed at her. Any delay might mean another death— possibly her own.

After what seemed an hour, but according to the mantel clock had been less than ten minutes, Jared returned.

"Did he give you a lead?" She barely allowed him time to sit.

Jared propped his elbows on the table and raked his fingers through his hair. When he lifted his head, she read the disappointment in his face.

"The warden remembered Ozzie Anderson, all right. Called him the meanest snake in a pit of vipers."

She leaned forward with excitement. "Then it's possible Ozzie *did* persuade another inmate to carry out his revenge killing for him?"

Jared shook his head. "Ozzie's crimes were so terrible, the other inmates hated him. He spent most of his time in isolation, for his own protection."

"What about visitors, someone from the outside?"

"For the last five years Ozzie was on death row, he refused all visitors except his family and his lawyer." Jared signaled the waitress and pointed to his empty coffee cup.

Tyler tried to make sense of the information. "That leaves the lawyer, Mrs. Anderson and Arnie Anderson as suspects."

"Forget the lawyer. He works for Amnesty International—not exactly the murdering type."

She remembered the woman at the farmhouse. "And all Mrs. Anderson wants is to be left alone."

Jared poured cream in his coffee. "That leaves Arnie. But the warden described him as quiet and shy, not eaten up with rage as his father had been."

"Not to mention that he's in Alaska."

Wearily, Jared pinched the bridge of his nose. "We're missing something. I can feel it."

She covered his hand with hers, luxuriating in the closeness. "We should pay Sam Witek another visit. With his skill as a detective, maybe he can point out what we've overlooked."

A THUNDERING HERD of elephants could have stampeded through their room during the night, and Jared wouldn't have heard them. The realization of how soundly he'd slept disturbed him as they headed back toward Roseland after lunch. Some protector he'd been. The only way to guarantee Tyler's safety was to send her back to her grandmother, which he intended to do as soon as they'd talked with Sam Witek again.

Sam glanced up in surprise when they entered his room. "Didn't think I'd be seeing you folks again. What did you find out from the warden?"

Sam's withered face creased in concentration as Jared filled him in on the warden's revelations.

"We've reached a dead end," Jared concluded, "and hope you can help us."

Sam pointed a trembling finger at the bookcase. "Hand me that photo album. Maybe some of those old pictures will jog my memory."

Jared lifted the album from the low bookshelf and set it on the bed next to Sam, who flipped it open.

Tyler watched over Sam's shoulder, and as he turned the second page, she gasped. Blood drained from her face and her eyes widened in horror as she pointed to the top photograph on the page.

"It's him." She forced a strangled whisper between wooden lips.

"Ozzie Anderson?" Sam squinted at the photo through his reading glasses. "It can't be. I don't have his picture."

"No." Tyler sank into the bedside chair as if her legs would no longer support her. "It's the man who drove the Blazer."

Sam extended the photo album to arm's length, studying the snapshot.

"I don't understand." Sam shook his head and struggled to breathe. "That's Pete Stanwick, taken the year before Mary died."

Chapter Ten

Tyler stared from the plane's window as the 747 descended into clouds obscuring the valley where the Asheville airport lay. The insides of her eyelids itched with fatigue after a sleepless night, and Jared snoozed in the seat beside her, surrendering to exhaustion.

He'd remained silent all the way back to the inn yesterday after their last visit with Sam Witek. The only words he'd spoken were instructions to Enrico to wait while he collected their luggage and checked out.

The trip back to Boston had been equally quiet. She hadn't encroached on his stillness, allowing him to contemplate uninterrupted the facts they'd uncovered. When they'd reached the airport, all direct flights to Asheville were booked, and Jared had bought tickets for the next morning.

Their battle royal had begun after they'd checked into the airport hotel.

Tyler had picked up the envelope Jared had placed on the bureau, scrutinized its contents, and confronted him with accusing eyes. "There's only one ticket here to Asheville. The other's to Raleigh-Durham."

"Tomorrow morning we part company," Jared announced with a coldness that froze her heart.

"Why? We know who the killer is. All we have to do is point the police in the right direction."

He grabbed her shoulders, and for an instant, she feared he would shake her. "Pete Stanwick's a former policeman, who knows law-enforcement procedures. If anybody can elude capture, he can. It could be a year or more before they bring him in."

Tyler ignored his too-tight hold and, reaching up, cupped his face in her hands, forcing him to meet her eyes. "Why are you so angry with me?"

His fierce expression melted. "I'm not angry. I just don't want anything to happen to you."

He pushed her hands away and strode to the window that overlooked the runway, where a jumbo jet taxied into the night, red lights flashing in the darkness. The rigid line of his back repelled her.

"Don't make this any harder than it already is," he muttered with a low groan.

The hardest part would be leaving him. Anger at his lack of comprehension surged through her. "Give me one good reason why I can't stay."

He whipped around and defied her with blazing eyes. "Because staying with me will get you killed."

She glared at him and raised her voice, heedless of guests in the adjoining rooms. "Not if we don't return to your mountaintop."

The low urgency of his words carried above the whine of the ascending jet. "I have to go back. Stanwick will be expecting me, and I'll set a trap for him there."

"With you as bait? Are you out of your mind?" Pain stabbed her at the thought of losing him. She was no longer halfway in love. She was totally committed, and she would move heaven and earth to keep him safe. "Tell the authorities what you know. Use your trust fund and move to Bermuda or the Bahamas until he's caught."

He stared past her shoulder, avoiding her eyes. "You're forgetting one crucial point."

Her breath caught in her throat at the defeat in his expression. "What point?"

"Stanwick has some kind of psychic link with me. He can find me, wherever I go."

"But—"

"That's why you have to leave. Stanwick's not after you. It's me he wants, and if you're not with me, you're safe."

"If I'm not with you, I'll—" she blurted, catching herself before she said too much.

His eyes burned into hers. "You'll what?"

He would probably laugh at her admission, but she couldn't help herself. "I'll wither up and die from missing you, wondering if you're safe."

"Tyler, no, don't—" He breathed her name like a prayer before covering the distance between them in two long strides and sweeping her into his arms. His mouth dipped hungrily to hers, and her senses swirled at the taste of him.

In the refuge of his arms, all thoughts of danger vanished, and the universe contracted to the space they occupied. Nothing else mattered. She twined her arms around his neck, pressing against the hard length of his body, reveling in the thunder of his heart against hers. Desire burgeoned within her, and every cell cried out in longing.

Abruptly, he lifted his mouth from hers and held her at arm's length. "This can't change anything."

His look of devastation gave her hope. "Don't send me away, Jared."

"It won't be for long—"

"You just said it could be over a year." A prolonged separation was too painful to contemplate.

"It might be only a few weeks." He cradled her face in his hands and brushed a wisp of hair off her forehead. "Would you wait that long for me?"

She shivered with delight at his touch and felt herself drowning in the warm brown depths of his eyes. She nodded, afraid to trust her voice.

He clasped her to him again, stroking her hair, pressing her cheek to the broad expanse of his chest. His deep voice rumbled in her ear. "We'll both be safer if you're with your grandmother."

She snuggled deeper into his embrace. "How will you be safer?"

"For one thing, I'll be less distracted." He lifted her hair and brushed the back of her neck with his lips.

She raised her head. "I couldn't bear it if anything happened to you."

"Then promise me you'll go to your grandmother's." Fierce protectiveness lighted his eyes.

Torn between reluctance to leave him and desire to keep him safe, she nodded. He'd made it clear he wouldn't allow her to stay. "But only if I can fly back with you and pick up my car."

"No—"

"I promise I won't stay. Just get in my car and leave." She would promise anything to remain with him for as long as possible.

He appraised her with raised eyebrows. "Do you always get your way?"

"Not as often as I'd like."

"Like now?"

She nodded, unable to catch her breath beneath the intensity of his gaze.

He traced her cheek with his fingertip. "What is it you want?"

"A night to remember while we're apart."

In answer, he claimed her mouth in a deep, endless kiss as he scooped her into his arms and carried her to the king-size bed. She pushed her fingers through his fine, thick hair as she savored the taste of him, a tantalizing sensation that sparked a deep hunger.

He laid her on the bed, and she tilted her head, exposing her throat to his soft, sliding kisses. He tugged her sweater over her head, then gently unfastened the buttons of her blouse. With every pulse point awakened, her body arched toward his.

A sigh exploded from the depths of him, and he hovered above her, his face clouded. "This is a mistake."

His words stunned her like a torrent of cold rain. "I thought you wanted this, too."

"If you only knew how much." The heat of his hands seared her bare shoulders, and his face darkened with irony. "I've loved you since *before* I met you."

"That's not possible."

"I loved you in my dream."

That same dream had predicted her death. She thrust aside the thought. Nothing, no one would spoil this night. "If you love me, how can this be a mistake?"

"This close, I can't remain objective." He levered himself away. "If I drop my guard, Stanwick might—"

"Tomorrow you can be objective." She pulled him toward her and tugged his shirt from his jeans, unbuttoned it, and ran her palms across his chest.

He trembled at her touch, then caught her hands and forced them away. "If I make love to you now, I may not be able to let you go tomorrow."

Her heart ached at the caring shining in his eyes. She must have done something right in her short life to have earned the love of such a man. More than his classic good looks and sexy body, his integrity, intelligence and deep-rooted compassion attracted her, binding her to him like velvet chains.

"I give you my word." Her solemn tone echoed in the quiet room. "I'll leave tomorrow, just as you asked."

"Tyler."

He breathed her name against her breasts as he knelt beside her, pressing his lips against her heartbeat. With slow, reverent gestures, he slipped off her shoes, tugged away her jeans, and stripped away her bra and panties. Hypnotizing her with his stare, he removed his clothes and lay down beside her, pulling her against him.

His flesh warmed her in the air-conditioned coolness, and the hardness of his arousal thrust against her thigh. So tightly were their bodies entwined, she couldn't tell if his muscles quivered or her own. Slowly, he released her shoulders and trailed his strong hands across her breasts and her waist, then skimmed her hips and sought the small secret center of her being, lingering there.

Her body tensed and throbbed, drifting on a rising current of ecstasy until she soared with a roaring in her ears like a jet climbing to the heavens.

"Jared," she murmured, as he lifted himself above her, cradled her head in one hand, and with the other, opened her thighs and surged inside her.

A moan escaped her lips, and she clung to him, digging her fingers into his shoulders, fearing she might die of pleasure. His gaze locked with hers before he lowered his mouth, wet and hot, to her lips. He moved in slow, languorous thrusts until the tide of bliss crested again in her, merging with his, washing away all other thoughts except love for the man who created it.

Later she lay cradled in his arms as he sat against the headboard in the darkened room, watching planes take off and land at the distant airport.

"I won't let anyone harm you," he promised. "Not ever."

She pressed her fingers to his lips. "Don't think about anything but here and now."

That here and now had passed too quickly. Now, in the cramped confines of the airplane cabin, she sighed, remembering how they had made love again, leaving only a couple of hours for sleep before rushing to catch the morning flight to Asheville.

"Ladies and gentlemen," the flight attendant's voice interrupted, "we'll be landing in Asheville in a few minutes. Please fasten your seat belts."

As Tyler secured her lap harness, Jared grasped her hand and lifted her palm to his lips. "Happy landings."

She wondered if anyone ever died from the sheer happiness of love and wished she hadn't promised she would leave. He'd been right. Deserting him now would be twice as hard after their lovemaking, but she would keep her word. She had no other choice.

JARED CROSSED TO A BANK of pay phones in the air terminal, dropped in a quarter, and dialed. "Sheriff Tillett, please."

"The sheriff? Won't he be looking for us?" Tyler hissed.

He covered the mouthpiece with his hand. "Maybe, but we have to take that chance."

She stood with her fists on her hips in defiance, one hundred pounds of adorable trouble. "But what if—"

A voice sounded in his ear and he jerked his hand from the mouthpiece. "Sheriff, Jared Slater here. I'm calling about the shot that was fired at my house a few days ago."

"I've had some boys from Florida inquiring about you, Slater." Tillett's drawling voice boomed in his ear. "What's going on?"

"More than I can relate in a short phone call," Jared replied. "But the same man who fired the shots ran me off the road in Georgia, and he may still be after me."

Tillett harrumphed. "That's not the way the Florida boys tell it. Seems you're wanted for questioning about a murder down there."

Jared squinted and pinched the bridge of his nose, willing away his fatigue. "I'll be happy to answer any questions once I get home. I'm leaving the airport now. How about having your deputies check out my place before I get there?"

"And what should I tell them to look for?" the sheriff asked.

"The man who's after me is Pete Stanwick, an ex-cop from Massachusetts in his late fifties, tall, graying hair, heavy build."

"Do you know what he's driving?" Tillett asked.

"Not a clue, except it's probably a rental car of some kind." The sound of Tillett's scribbling carried over the line. "Tell them the man's dangerous and clever. Stanwick might not miss this time, if he's still around."

Tillett sighed, as if dealing with a naughty child. "I'll send Darwin and McSwain to check out your place, then I'll be there myself in a couple of hours. I expect you to be waiting for me."

"Thanks." Jared relaxed his death grip on the phone. "I'll be there."

DRAGGING HIS SUITCASES, Jared climbed the stairs to his bedroom. For two years, he'd lived alone in his mountain retreat, and it had never felt so empty as it did now.

When he'd driven the rental car up to his door just minutes earlier, Deputy McSwain had been waiting for them.

"No sign of your Mr. Stanwick," McSwain had said. "No sign of anybody, for that matter. We've checked all the roads, and I'll set up a watch at the foot of the mountain until the sheriff gets here."

Sunlight shimmered on the new leaves of the surrounding trees, and a cardinal chirped in the distance. Everything seemed peaceful enough, and with a deputy blocking the road, the only way Stanwick could reach the mountaintop was to climb the escarpment behind the house. Unless Stanwick was a mountain goat, he would never make it.

The deputy had backed his cruiser around and eased down the drive, leaving Jared alone with Tyler in the cool spring air.

He fumbled in his pocket for his keys, unable to face her, knowing it might be for the last time, if Stanwick wasn't stopped. He longed to scoop her into his arms, carry her up to his loft bed and make love to her until they were both exhausted, but reason conquered his emotions. His most important responsibility was to send her out of harm's way.

After he unlocked the garage, she unlatched the trunk of her car and he stowed her luggage. Silence stretched between them like a fragile pane of glass both were afraid to shatter.

She slammed the trunk lid and turned to him. Tears sparkled in her eyes, and the smile she flashed seemed a valiant attempt at bravery. "Will you be all right?"

He kept his hands at his sides, quashing his desire to embrace her. If he kissed her again, he wouldn't be able to let her leave. "I'll be fine. The sheriff will be here soon, and I'll tell him everything."

Her brow creased with worry. "Even your dreams?"

He shrugged. He would bare his soul to the world, if needed, to put Stanwick behind bars so she could safely return. "None of it makes sense without the dreams."

She smiled through her tears. "As if they make sense."

"Goodbye, Tyler." He choked out the words past the lump in his throat. "Be careful."

She slid into her car and rolled down the window. "I'll call you when I reach Gran's."

He had watched until her car had disappeared among the trees, then carried his luggage inside.

As he unpacked in his bedroom, he shivered in the loft's damp chill, a stark contrast to the warmth outdoors. But it matched the feeling in his heart.

Tires crunched on his gravel driveway—the sheriff was early. He stowed the last of his clothes in the closet.

"Jared?" Tyler's voice floated up to him.

He glanced over the loft wall to find her standing in the center of the room. In a horrific case of déjà vu, through the high windows he spied sunlight streaming over the early blooms of rhododendron on the mountainside.

And saw the priority envelope in her hand.

Chapter Eleven

Immobilized by his worst nightmare coming true, Jared couldn't force his feet to move.

She smiled at him with a hint of chagrin. "I'm just dropping off your mail. The priority envelope marked Urgent was in your mailbox. It looks important."

Her words prodded him into action. He raced across the loft, screaming as he moved. "No!"

From the top of the stairway, he lunged, landing beside her. He wrenched the envelope from her hand and tossed it, Frisbee-style, out the open front door. In the same movement, he knocked her to the floor, covering her body with his own.

An earsplitting explosion rocked the mountaintop, shaking the timbers of the house, raining glass down from the tall windows, and jarring his bones.

When the last reverberation faded, he lifted himself to his feet, shedding shards of glass. On the braided rug beneath him, Tyler lay sprawled on her back, her wide eyes unblinking, with a bleeding gash in her forehead—just as he had dreamed.

His agonized cry split the silence as he fell to his knees and gathered her motionless body into his arms. "Oh, God, Tyler, no. . ."

A long, choking wheeze sounded against his ear as she convulsed in his arms. He pulled back, slid his hands to her shoulders, and stared. Her face crumpled in distress as she fought for air.

He skimmed his hands over her, searching for injuries, but she struggled against him, trying to sit up.

"Where are you hurt?" he demanded.

She shook her head, still laboring to breathe. He raced to the kitchen for a towel and returned to press it to the wound on her forehead.

"Hold this—" he raised her hand to the towel "—I'll call an ambulance."

She clutched the compress to her head and sucked in a deep, gasping breath. "I'm okay. You just knocked the wind out of me when you tackled me."

"Are you sure?" Joy mixed with anxiety. He hadn't lost her as he'd feared, and he would be damned if he let anything happen to her now. "Won't you need stitches?"

She withdrew the towel. "Looks like the bleeding's almost stopped. If you'll just help me up—"

He lifted her to her feet, guided her to the sofa, and settled beside her, gathering her into his arms and murmuring against the softness of her hair. "The priority envelope, the sunshine, the explosion were exactly like in my dream. Only in my dream—"

"I died?" Cupping his cheek in her palm, she studied him with a worried frown.

He nodded and tightened his arms around her. His world had stopped when she'd reappeared in the great room, and in that instant, he had feared he'd lost her forever.

She pushed away from his chest and stared at him, excitement dancing in her eyes. "But that's good."

"Good?" There had been nothing good about his scare. His heart still bludgeoned his chest like a jackhammer.

She wiggled from his embrace and stood with her hands on her hips. "Not good that I died in the dream. Good that the dream didn't come true."

The significance of her words struck him. "My dreams *aren't* inevitable."

She nodded, then returned to his arms and snuggled against him. "And I don't ever have to leave you again."

Her luminous eyes made promises beyond words. No woman had ever looked at him that way, and he fought for breath against the unaccustomed pressure in his chest. He grazed her silky throat with his lips and worked his way upward toward the sweetness of her mouth, pouring out his love, reveling in her acceptance.

Tires skidded to a halt on the drive, and reluctantly he released her and rose to meet the arrivals. A wild-eyed McSwain strode through the open door, followed by Sheriff Tillett, whose beefy face glowed red.

"What the hell happened out there?" Tillett demanded.

Jared raked his hands through his hair. "Letter bomb."

"Holy—" Catching sight of Tyler, Tillett squelched his curse and turned to his deputy. "Get on the radio and request the postal inspectors. And notify the FBI and ATF while you're at it."

As McSwain rushed out the door, Tillett swiveled back to Jared. "Now, Mr. Slater, you have a lot of explaining to do. Who blasted a hole the size of a swimming pool in your front yard?"

Tyler picked up the blood-stained towel and scooted toward the kitchen. "It's a long story, Sheriff. I'll make some coffee."

Tillett grasped her arm as she passed. "You okay? Every time I see you, you've been knocked on the head."

Her face twisted in an ironic smile. "Occupational hazard, but I'm fine."

Jared's heart swelled with pride at her spirit. She was even braver than he'd assumed when he first met her. No wonder he loved her.

He gestured the sheriff toward a chair and sat opposite him. "I don't know how much you'll believe, but I'd appreciate if you'd listen to the whole story."

Tillett nodded, and Jared launched into the tale of his strange dreams, leaving nothing out—from his first dream in the hospital, to their final visit with Sam Witek in the Massachusetts nursing home.

When Jared finished, Tillett refused more coffee from Tyler and set aside his cup. "A year ago, I'd have thought you had a screw loose, Slater, but, by God, I believe you're telling the truth."

"What makes you so willing to accept my story?" Jared had feared the pragmatic Tillett would be the last person to give credence to his dreams.

The sheriff tugged at the starched collar of his uniform. "Last summer a young couple down by the lake lost their four-year-old boy when he wandered off into the woods. We rounded up a search party of over a hundred volunteers and combed the mountainside. Twenty-four hours later, we'd found no trace of him."

"Was he kidnapped?" Tyler asked.

"That's what we feared," the sheriff said. "But the kid's mother refused to believe it. She contacted a psychic in Virginia Beach and flew her here to help our search. I considered psychics either charlatans or weirdos—"

Jared winced at the description.

"But I figured if she helped calm the boy's mother, what harm could she do?" Tillett's lips curved in a self-effacing grin. "The psychic arrived—a little old lady in tennis shoes who reminded me of my grandmother. Within two hours, she led us straight to the child, asleep under a rock ledge on a sector of the mountain we'd already searched. Damnedest thing I've ever seen in all my years of law enforcement."

"Then you'll go after Stanwick?" Tyler asked. "The bomb had to come from him. He must have sent it after he lost track of us when we flew to Massachu-setts.''

"We'll bring him in for questioning," Tillett prom-ised. He cocked his head at the hum of vehicles ap-proaching. "That must be the federal boys and their forensics crew now."

"I'll make sandwiches," Tyler said, "and more coffee. Looks like it's going to be a long afternoon."

PETE STANWICK STOOD in front of the cold drink compartment of the grocery at the foot of the moun-tain and studied his altered appearance in the glass door. Brown dye covered his gray-streaked black hair, a close shave had removed all traces of his beard, and aviator sunglasses hid his bloodshot eyes.

He removed a can of Mountain Dew from the cooler and carried it to the checkout counter. He was the only customer in the store.

"You from outta town?" the young man at the cash register asked in a making-conversation tone.

"Raleigh," Stanwick lied.

"Kinda early in the season for tourists." The clerk rang up the soda.

Stanwick handed him a five. "I'm not on vacation. I'm a botanist at N.C. State. Been collecting wild-flower specimens up the mountain."

"You and half the county been on that mountain today." The clerk counted out his change.

"I noticed the sheriff's cars and some other offi-cial-looking vehicles." Stanwick nodded at the scanner radio on the shelf behind the clerk. "You know what's going on?"

The clerk folded his arms on the counter and leaned forward conspiratorially. "Most excitement we've had in years. Somebody got a mail bomb. Blew away a chunk of the mountaintop."

"No kidding." Stanwick made a sympathetic clucking sound. "Anybody hurt?"

"Not that I can tell from the scanner, and I haven't seen an ambulance—or a hearse."

Stanwick glanced down at his Mountain Dew, where his tightened fist dented the can. Slater had more lives than a cat, but even a cat had to die sometime. He reached into his pocket for the keys of the battered pickup he'd stolen in north Georgia and headed toward the door.

"Hey, mister," the clerk called.

Startled, Stanwick halted. "Yeah?"

"You come back now, you hear?"

IN THE GLARE OF THE outside floodlights, Tyler watched Jared nail a plywood panel over the last of the gaping holes where glass had once been. The concussion of the blast had shattered every window in the house, including the small panes in the French doors leading to the loft balcony.

She thrust away thoughts of the recent explosion and her close call with death, concentrating on Jared's skill with tools, and the fluid grace of the bare muscles of his torso as he hefted sheets of plywood and wielded his hammer. She hadn't expected such proficiency from a journalist, but Jared continued to surprise her with his talents.

"That should keep out rain and cold until the glass is replaced." He tucked the hammer into his tool belt, climbed over the balcony railing and descended the ladder.

"If you don't mind sleeping in a cave," Tyler observed.

"Where's your sense of romance?" he teased as he shrugged on his shirt against the encroaching chill. "We can have candlelight at noon under these conditions."

Her thoughts took a more practical turn. "And we'll be safer, boarded up like Fort Knox."

He flung an arm around her shoulders and hugged her close as they circled to the front of the house. "We have our personal bodyguard, remember?"

He pointed to the deputy, stationed in the cruiser parked across the drive, before gathering his power saw and plywood scraps and stowing them in the garage.

She avoided the sight of the gaping hole and broken tree trunks on the mountainside, circled by fluttering yellow police tape. She'd come close to dying today, at a time when she'd discovered she had everything to live for. Her happiness with Jared, fueled by his love, seemed too perfect to last, and she wouldn't rest easy until Pete Stanwick was behind bars, no longer a threat to the man she loved.

She followed Jared into the house. "Stanwick has to find out sooner or later that the bomb didn't harm you. What will he do then?"

He smoothed back her hair. "Authorities all over the eastern half of the country are searching for him. Unless he's invisible, they'll catch him soon."

"I hope you're right." She sagged against him, wrung dry of emotion and energy by the events of the day.

He enfolded her in a rough embrace before scooping her into his arms. "It's late and you're exhausted. I'm putting you to bed."

Encircling his neck with her arms, she leaned back and studied his face, her lips quirked in a flirtatious smile. "That's the nicest thing you've said all day."

He carried her up the loft stairs and placed her on the bed. "While you get out of those clothes, I'll bring up your bags."

When she came out of the bathroom minutes later, her suitcases rested on a chest at the foot of the bed, and he'd laid her warm gown across the pillow. She tossed the clothes she'd removed across a chair, slipped into the flannel gown, and slid between the sheets. The comforting weight of Jared on the other side of the bed registered vaguely on her consciousness before she drifted into a sound sleep.

She awakened to pitch-darkness and a hand over her mouth.

"Keep quiet—" Jared's lips moved against her ear "—and get dressed—quick!"

She scrambled to the foot of the bed, groped for her clothes and jerked them on with trembling hands. Over the rush of blood in her ears, she detected scratching sounds at the front door, as if someone attempted to force the lock.

As she searched the floor for her second shoe, she sensed Jared's presence before he leaned close again.

"The phone's dead," he whispered, "so we can't call for help."

"What about the deputy?" She winced when her voice sounded louder than she'd intended.

"If it's Stanwick out there—" He left her to her own conclusions. "Find your sweater."

She tied the last shoelace and fumbled for her pullover. "Do you have a gun?"

He grabbed her hand and touched it to the pistol in his belt. "He may not give me a chance to use it. Our best bet is to run."

The scratching sound at the front door ceased.

She jerked her hand from the weapon. "But if Stanwick's outside, where do we run?"

"Where he least expects us."

Disoriented by the darkness, she allowed him to guide her. When a crack of light glimmered, she recognized the balcony door. Jared pushed her through it, stepped onto the deck in the faint moonlight, and closed the door behind him.

"There." He pointed with a whisper to the ladder he'd used to install the plywood. "Down you go."

She hung back, gripping his arm, while dark fear gnawed at her insides. "I forgot to tell you—I'm afraid of heights."

"I'll go first and stay right behind you. You'll be fine." He swung over the railing onto the ladder. "Come on."

The thought of confronting Pete Stanwick propelled her onto the ladder, but once she was suspended on the precarious perch a story above the ground, she froze with panic. She tried to reassure herself, but perspiration slicked her palms, and mental images of falling through nothingness consumed her.

"Easy." Jared moved up behind her, his arms bracing hers, his chest pressing against her buttocks. "Breathe deep, move with me, and don't look down."

Soothed by his presence, she inched her way down, exhaling with relief when her feet hid solid ground.

Jared pointed to a dense stand of evergreens at the back of his lot. "Run for cover and wait for me."

"But—"

"Do it!" He shoved her toward the trees.

She ran, stumbling over the uneven earth, terrified that at any moment Stanwick would appear to gun down Jared, who stood exposed in the open yard.

When she reached the trees, she plunged into the thick branches, where the resinous scent of pine filled her nostrils, battling with the coppery stench of fear. She peered through the cover of evergreen toward the house. Jared's shadowy figure blurred against the house as he moved toward a shed by the back door. He disappeared inside.

Seconds seemed to stretch into hours while she waited. When Jared slipped from the shed and dashed across the yard with a murky bundle across his shoulders, she expelled the breath she'd been holding. He crashed into the branches and dropped his burden at her feet.

"What's that?" she whispered.

"Our ticket out of here." He pulled on a pair of heavy gloves, fastened some kind of harness around his hips, and hefted his bundle again. "Come on. We're running out of time."

She followed him a few yards through the trees into a clearing. Behind her, the evergreen forest formed a dark barrier between them and the house. Before her, a rock cliff, a sheer fall of over sixty feet, dropped toward the valley. Her head swam dizzily from the height, and her stomach clutched with nausea.

In the clearing's bright moonlight, she identified the nylon rope looped over Jared's shoulder. He fastened it to a stanchion at the cliff's edge and unfurled it. With disturbing fascination, she watched it drop down the cliffside.

"I'll tie you to me," he said, "and we can rappel down together."

"Are you crazy?" she hissed. "I could barely force myself to climb down a ladder, and you expect me to dive off a cliff?"

She flinched as bursts of gunfire erupted behind them in the house, and a man's angry shouts echoed in the night.

"We have two choices," Jared said. "Go over the cliff or face Stanwick. Which will it be?"

Paralyzed by apprehension, she couldn't answer.

He seized her face in his gloved hands. "You have to trust me, Tyler."

His love gave her strength. She would trust him with her life. She choked back a sob.

"The cliff," she agreed.

He knelt with his back to her and she climbed on, wrapping her arms around his neck and her legs around his waist. With quick, practiced movements, he lashed her to him.

Standing with an ease that testified to the strength of his legs, he strode to the cliff edge and grasped the rope. "Don't look down."

She stifled an hysterical laugh. She wasn't about to look down or anywhere else. She hid her face in his neck. In the next instant, she was hurtling through space.

Oh, God, she thought. *The rope isn't holding and we're plummeting to the cliff base.*

Just as she opened her lips to scream, the impact of Jared's feet against the rock face jolted her.

"You're doing fine," he assured her. "This won't take long. I've done it hundreds of times, then I practice climbing back to the top."

Again they fell through emptiness, with the rope sliding through Jared's gloves. His boots thudded against the cliff wall as he pushed off for another plunge, and air whistled past them as they dropped. Above, the patter of gunfire continued.

With each stage of the descent, Tyler's heart leaped to her throat, threatening to bang its way out of her body.

"What's he shooting at?" she whispered as Jared paused to push off.

"Don't know, but let's hope he keeps it up."

"Why?"

"As long as he's shooting up the house, he hasn't found the stanchion that holds the rope."

Dizzy with fright, she gripped Jared tighter, thankful for the harness that bound her to him. But if Stanwick sawed the line Jared held, they would both pitch to their deaths on the rocks below.

"We're almost there." His words came in small pants as he gasped from exertion.

He shoved away from the escarpment again, and they sank like stones. After what seemed an eternity in free fall, Jared's boots struck the ground, jarring Tyler's bones. With a swift movement, he untied the restraint that lashed her to him, and she slid onto the ground in a heap, her muscles quivering with relief.

Pulling hand-over-hand, Jared reined in the line from the mountainside, coiled the rope and stashed it in a clump of rhododendron. "No need to let Stanwick know how we escaped."

He lifted her to her feet and she leaned into him, reveling in the solid warmth of his arms and the sensation of firm ground beneath her shoes. She had trusted him, and he had brought her to safety.

"What now?" she asked.

He brushed a too-quick kiss across her lips. "We find a phone to alert the authorities. We'll have to hike to Sweeney's farm in the valley."

The trembling in her legs had eased. "I'm ready—"

A buzzing whine erupted on the boulder beside her as a bullet ricocheted, and rock chips stung her face.

"I'll get you, Slater! You can't run from me!" The tortured scream drifted down from the top of the cliff and echoed across the valley. Above Jared and Tyler, moonlight silhouetted an ominous shadow.

They ran into the cover of the forest just as Stanwick fired into the surrounding foliage, emptying his gun. The close call made Tyler giddy.

"We're not safe yet. Keep low and keep moving." Jared shoved her ahead, deeper into the trees.

Branches whipped her face, and crawling vines clutched at her feet as she stumbled to keep up with him. When the terrain descended sharply, she sat, scooting on her bottom down the steep slopes, brushing dogwood foliage from her path. When she slowed, Jared matched his pace to hers.

After endless hiking, she collapsed beside a tiny creek that bubbled down the mountainside to the lake, and cupped icy water in her hands to drink and to cool her heated cheeks. Drying her hands on her jeans, she massaged her aching calves. ''Why don't we use the road?''

Jared stooped on the mossy bank and splashed his face with the frigid water. ''Too easy for Stanwick to spot us in the open.''

She nodded. She'd survived the cliff descent, battling her worst fears. She could struggle through the rhododendron a few more miles.

He rose and offered his hand, pulling her to her feet and against him in one motion. The fierceness of his embrace drove the breath from her body. ''I won't let him harm you, Tyler, I promise.''

Determination glinted in the brown depths of his eyes. She traced the sharp angle of his jaw with her palm. ''I've caught my breath now. We'd better keep moving.''

He pointed to a narrow earthen path that wound down the slope beside the stream, and she lunged ahead. Behind them, something heavy crashed through the underbrush, shattering the nocturnal quiet.

''Stanwick?'' she breathed.

''Sounds like a bear,'' Jared whispered. ''But it's headed away from us.''

Adrenaline provided a burst of speed, and she darted forward along the trail, digging in her heels to avoid pitching down the incline. Jared followed close behind.

Her legs ached from exertion, and her breath came in tortured gasps. Long hours hunched over a desk and computer had drained her stamina. When she thought her lungs would explode if she lifted another foot, light glimmered ahead. They'd reached Sweeney's meadow at the bottom of the mountain.

Jared gripped her arm and pulled her back into the shadows before she ventured into the open. "If Stanwick drove, he could be waiting for us."

He dropped to his knees and propped the bottom skein of barbed wire with a stick. "Crawl under, then follow me."

She rolled beneath the wire, crushing the sweet spring grass beneath her, filling the air with the scent of herbs and wild onion. Jared copied her movements, then wriggled forward on his hands and knees, ducking his head below the level of the tall grass.

Tyler bit back a scream when the plaintive moo of a nearby cow startled her, but she kept crawling, close on Jared's heels. The aromatic clover thinned, then disappeared in a muddy yard. They had reached the barn.

Jared pushed to his feet, dragged her upright, and, still grasping her arm, sprinted toward the barn door. He slid back the massive door and yanked her into the cavernous darkness.

Groping through the shadows, she located a bale of hay and tumbled onto it, winded and exhausted. "Why stop here? Why not go on to the house and wake up Sweeney?"

Jared remained at the door, which was opened a crack to the moonlight. "I have to make certain Stanwick didn't get here first."

"How can you tell?"

His gaze swiveled, taking in the farmhouse and yard. "There's no sign of another vehicle. Just Sweeney's run-down old pickup."

Suddenly, blinding light flooded the barn from overhead fixtures, and Tyler blinked in the brightness. At the far end beneath the hayloft stood Pete Stanwick, his semiautomatic rifle trained on them.

"What took you so long?" he asked.

Chapter Twelve

Jared cursed himself for a fool. He'd underestimated Stanwick—a fatal error. Inching slowly toward Tyler, he intended to shield her with his body, giving her a chance to run.

"How did you find us?" he asked.

The night-vision goggles attached to Stanwick's belt answered his question, but Jared needed to keep his assailant talking while he formed a plan.

Stanwick tapped the side of his nose with an index finger. "I'm a good detective." His face clouded. "At least, I used to be."

"You sent the bomb to my house?" Jared demanded.

Stanwick shook his head, as if in disbelief. "I can't understand how you dodged that bullet. You don't have a scratch."

"No thanks to you," Tyler said.

Stanwick considered her for a moment before turning back to Jared. His eyes gleamed with suspicion. "And you survived that car crash, too. You got some kind of pact with the devil, Slater, that keeps you whole?''

''What have you done with the Sweeneys, and the deputy on the mountaintop?'' Tyler asked.

She leaned back on the hay bale and crossed her legs, and Jared admired her coolness. If she was as terrified as he, she didn't show it.

''I didn't hurt them,'' Stanwick said with a low growl. ''Just tied 'em up and gagged 'em. It's Slater I want.''

Jared reached the hay bale and slid down beside Tyler, prepared to fling himself in front of her if Stanwick fired. ''Why me?''

Stanwick grimaced, and in the chill of the barn, sweat rolled down his face, streaking it with brown hair dye. ''You know too damn much, Slater.''

''I know all about you, Stanwick,'' Jared agreed with a nod as he shifted his right arm behind him. He grasped the butt of his pistol, which was tucked in his belt at the small of his back. ''Except why you killed Veronica Molinsky and Evelyn Granger.''

Insanity glittered in Pete's glazed eyes. ''Why not? If my Mary had to die, why should anybody else live?''

Jared eased the pistol from his belt at his back. ''What about your son?''

Stanwick's expression softened. ''Robby?''

Jared nodded. ''He's worried about you. He told us so.''

Graying stubble framed his wistful smile. "You saw my Robby?"

"He's a good-looking boy." Tyler's voice, calm and soothing, produced a visible effect as tears joined the sweat on Stanwick's face. "He was studying for his exams. You must be very proud of him."

When Stanwick lifted the drooping muzzle of the rifle, Jared tensed, ready to spring.

Pete studied the gun in his hands with a confused expression, and when he raised his head, his expression was that of a lost little boy. "Where is Robby? Is he here?"

"Put the gun down, Pete." Jared strained to keep his voice level while his body hummed on alert. "Don't you want to see your son again?"

"My son? I have a son?" His voice rang with amazement. He sank to his knees in the straw, grasping the barrel and lowering the gun butt onto the barn's dirt floor. His grinning face and puzzled voice indicated he'd severed his final thread with reality. "Ah, Mary, darling, you gave me a son."

"Robby will be glad to see you," Tyler assured him.

Jared aimed his pistol at Pete and slipped off the safety. With measured steps, he crossed the floor and removed the rifle from Stanwick's hands. "It's over now, Pete."

Stanwick focused on Jared's gun and queried in a childlike voice, "No more killing?"

"No more killing," Jared replied.

"THE MAN'S CRAZY as a coot," Sheriff Tillett observed, as his deputies ducked Stanwick's head and loaded him, handcuffed and shackled, into the back seat of a cruiser. "He lost touch with the real world a long time ago."

Jared nodded. "Insanity's the only explanation for three senseless killings."

Sadness underlined Tillett's grin. "You ought to have my job. Sometimes I think the whole world's crazy."

Tyler stepped off the front porch where she had watched with the Sweeneys as Stanwick was driven away, and linked her arm through Jared's. "Thanks for talking to the cops in Florida. In fact, thanks for everything, Sheriff."

The big man leaned forward and examined her face in the dawn light. "That's a good sign."

"What?" Tyler asked.

Tillett jerked his thumb toward her forehead. "The worst must be over. No new head wounds."

Jared threw a protective arm around her shoulders. "Never again."

Tillett nodded toward his cruiser. "I'll give you a ride up the mountain."

JARED HELPED TYLER from the back seat of the sheriff's car, and when she stumbled with fatigue, he grabbed her elbow to steady her. She didn't speak as they walked toward the front door.

"Thanks for your help." He paused at the entrance and shook Sheriff Tillett's hand.

"I should thank you. You did all the dirty work." With a silent salute, Tillett returned to his car.

Jared eased the door shut, flipped on a light against the dark interior, and followed Tyler up the loft stairs to the bedroom where bullet holes pockmarked the walls—the only remnant of Stanwick's presence.

Tyler sank onto the rumpled covers and was asleep when her head hit the pillow. Gently, Jared unlaced her sneakers and slipped off her socks. Blisters glowed on the backs of both her heels, but she hadn't complained once during the long descent of the mountainside.

His heart constricted as he recalled how close he'd come to losing her. Only luck had prevented Stanwick from blowing them both away. He smoothed her hair away from her face, picking out entangled twigs and leaves, then tugged her jeans over her hips, exposing long graceful legs. With a tender pull, he hauled her sweater over her head, then drew the covers over her. He couldn't tell if fatigue or passion caused his quivering.

She rolled onto her side, moaning softly in her sleep.

Staggering with exhaustion, he stripped down to his shorts and fell into bed beside her, circling her waist and drawing the warmth of her bare skin against him. Weariness battled his passion and won.

Hours later, a warm breeze tickled his nose, awakening him from a sound sleep. He opened his eyes to sunlight streaming into the room. Tyler had folded back the plywood-covered outer doors and stood on the balcony, barefoot, clad only in her blouse and underwear, gazing out over the valley.

He flung back the covers and went to her, wrapping his arms around her waist and drawing her close against him. "Feeling better?"

"Mmm." She snuggled deeper into his embrace. "Except for the aching muscles in my legs."

Happiness, an emotion he'd seldom experienced since his surgery, consumed him. In the sparkling air, cleared of its usual smoky haze, the valley stretched before him, picture-perfect, and with Tyler in his arms, he could think of nothing else necessary to make his life complete.

She turned to him, lifting her face to study him with anxious eyes. "Are *you* all right?"

He pressed a gentle kiss to her mouth. "If I were any more all right, I couldn't stand it."

"No more dreams?"

"Only erotic ones," he said with a grin.

She swatted him playfully on the shoulder. "Rappelling down the mountain, playing you-Tarzan, me-Jane, terrified me, but I think you actually enjoyed it."

She would never know how afraid he had been for her safety. From now on, he vowed silently, he would allow nothing ever to terrify her again.

He clasped her to him. "I know an old jungle remedy for aching muscles."

Before she could protest, he swung her over his shoulder and carried her into the bathroom, and her crystal laughter tickled his ear.

Balancing her on his shoulder, while she beat her fists on his back in mock protest, he turned on the hot water and adjusted the pulsating shower head before sliding her to her feet.

Her gaze locked with his while he unfastened the buttons of her blouse and pushed aside the fabric. She caught her breath with a hiss of delight and her eyes glowed with pleasure when he cupped her breasts, teasing the peaks with his thumbs.

He stripped off his shorts, then hooked his thumbs in her wispy panties and tugged them to the floor. As she stepped out of them, she shrugged the blouse from her shoulders.

His throat ached with joy. "You're beautiful."

She arched a feathery eyebrow above a teasing smile. "And you lured me here under false pretenses."

He threw back his head and pounded his chest in his best ape-man imitation. "Tarzan no lie."

He lifted her off her feet again and deposited her on the bench in the tiled shower stall. After adjusting the spray against her legs, he knelt and massaged her calves while the warm water pounded them.

She leaned back against the tile, a rapturous smile on her lips and water beading the silken smoothness of her skin, as he kneaded her muscles. "That's heavenly," she uttered with a soft moan.

Her pleasure filled him with delight. When he raised his hands to her thighs, she leaned toward him, and he buried his face between her breasts, pressing his lips to her heart as the pulsating water poured over them.

Her hands trailed over the muscles of his back and grazed his neck and shoulders, fueling the fire deep in his groin. He lifted his head and her eyes mirrored his passion. Then he stood, rigid with desire, pulled her to him and lifted her hips over him.

She wrapped her legs around his waist, drawing him deeper within her. Her lips melded with his, hot with longing, as she tightened her body around him. Awash in sensation, he clung to her with violent tenderness. Rapture erupted in waves and the pulsing water echoed the rhythms of his heart, buffeting their entwined bodies like a shower of stars.

Still cradling her, he sank to the bench as ecstasy receded, to be replaced by a lingering contentment. "I love you, Tyler."

She pushed his streaming hair from his eyes and fixed him with an expression that pierced him with desperate joy. "Love is forever, Jared."

"And a day." He claimed another kiss.

JARED WATCHED FROM the kitchen while Tyler arranged place settings on the table in front of the fire. Her black hair glistened in the soft light, and her cheeks, still tinged from lovemaking, glowed pink. His heart constricted with happiness, followed by a chill of fear. He'd come too close to losing her and their chance for a life together. Now that he'd committed himself to love, he must live with the risk such love entailed. Events of the past two years had taught him that nothing in life was guaranteed. Wondering where his somber thoughts had come from, he shook them off and carried the lasagna to the table.

Tyler inhaled the steam rising from the casserole, and her face crinkled in the smile he cherished. "That's why I fell in love with you," she said. "Who can resist a man who cooks?"

He settled at the table and reached across to grasp her hand. "Then you won't have any trouble saying yes to my request."

"More Tarzan games?" Her eyes glinted with humor.

He shook his head. "This is serious."

"I think I know." Her expression sobered and the light left her eyes. "Now that Stanwick's caught, you're firing me for good."

"In a manner of speaking." He struggled to keep a straight face.

She lifted her chin in a show of courage. "When do you want me to leave?"

He scooted around the table and drew her to him. "Never."

"But—"

"I'm firing you as my research assistant." He tilted her face toward his. "But I'm offering a permanent position instead."

"Permanent?"

He nodded. "Permanent, as in forever. I want you to marry me."

Her eyes brimmed with tears. "I love you, Jared."

Uncertainty stabbed him. "Is that a yes?"

Her arms tightened around his neck. "That is most definitely a yes."

"We'll take out a license tomorrow."

"Oh, no." Her eyes widened with dismay.

He clutched his heart in mock distress. "Don't do this to me, Tyler. You haven't changed your mind already, have you?"

"It's Gran."

"Will she object?" He'd been so estranged from his family, he'd forgotten about Tyler's.

"No, but I did make her a promise." Her expression wavered, and he couldn't read it.

"Please," he said with a groan, "you're not going to make me wait a year, or something equally excruciating?"

The corners of her mouth lifted in a wry smile. "Excruciating? Depends on how you feel about big weddings."

"Make the wedding as big or as small as you like," he answered with a delighted grin. "Just make it quick. The sooner I can have you all to myself, the better."

"We can leave first thing in the morning to break the news to Gran."

He frowned, remembering the makeshift repairs he'd made to the house. "I should meet with the contractor tomorrow to arrange for these windows to be replaced. That will give you a day to accustom her to the idea, and I'll join you day after tomorrow to meet her."

She grinned. "And to begin plans."

He nodded and gave a comical grimace. "A big wedding. Jeez, the things I do for love."

She traced his lips with her fingertips. "Yes, like saving my life."

Remembering her brushes with death, he fought against the huskiness in his throat. "We should eat. The lasagna's getting cold."

She nodded and accepted the heaping plate he handed her, but she didn't touch her food. "Something bothers me about Stanwick."

"What do you mean?" He dished out lasagna for himself.

She shrugged. "I'm not sure. Seeing him on his knees, all lost and confused, I felt sorry for him."

He dropped the serving spoon with a clang. "Tyler, the man tried to *kill* you."

"But he doesn't seem like a killer."

"The man's crazy. Besides, how many killers have you known?" He grinned and dug into his meal.

She blushed. "You're right, but I can't get him out of my mind."

"Believe me," he said with irony, "I know exactly how you feel. But he's haunted my dreams too long, and from now on, I intend to forget him."

She lifted her wineglass to his. "It's a deal. No more talk of Stanwick."

WHEN HE CLIMBED INTO BED that night, even Tyler's soft curves pressed against him like a nesting spoon couldn't erase Pete Stanwick from his mind. Something jiggled in the back of his consciousness, like a name he knew but couldn't remember. He squeezed his eyes shut and slowed his breathing, hoping that with Stanwick's murderous odyssey ended, their psychic connection had been broken and his own dreams would be normal once more.

He wasn't that lucky.

The vision gripped him, drawing him into the familiarity of the killer's mind, again drenching him in hate and vengeance. Through the killer's eyes, Jared observed the passing interstate, cutting through the North Carolina piedmont.

The killer drove, tailing a small compact car. The first vehicle turned into a rest area and the killer followed. Bitterness and murderous fever throbbed in the killer's mind, choking Jared with its intensity. He struggled to awaken, but he couldn't break his link with the killer's sick brain.

The killer parked and observed as a woman left the compact car at the other end of the deserted area and headed toward the rest rooms. He opened his door and hurried to the empty men's room. Inside, he withdrew a revolver from beneath his coat, flipped open the cylinder, and counted six rounds. More than enough to finish her off.

He bent over the lavatory, sloshed water over his heated face, and stood, staring into the mirror with vacant eyes. A vivid scar, obscured at his forehead by haylike hair, ran from his temple to his chin.

Jared fought again to waken.

The man stuffed the gun into his belt and stood at the door of the rest room, watching the ladies' room across the corridor. The woman stepped out, but her face was obscured. She hurried toward her car. The killer set off after her.

Exerting every effort to impose his will on the killer's, Jared battled with the killer's intent—to no avail. The enraged man continued his pursuit.

At the sound of running feet, the woman turned. The killer lifted his gun.

Jared awoke with a tortured scream on his lips. The killer was stalking Tyler.

And he was the same man who had sat across from Jared in the hospital, two years ago—just seconds before the aneurysm had burst in his brain.

Chapter Thirteen

Jared jammed a fist to his mouth to stifle his scream and squeezed his eyes shut. Forcing himself to inhale deep breaths, he attempted to relax.

It was just a dream.

A dream brought on by the stress of the last few days. Stanwick was behind bars and Tyler slept beside him, whole and safe.

Strange that after all this time he should dream about the man from the emergency room. But dreams seldom presented a reason for their existence, drawing out random experiences from the circuits of the brain, like a computer with a faulty program.

Logic eased Jared's terror. When his heart ceased hammering like a racing car piston, he rolled onto his side and reached for Tyler.

She was gone.

He bounded to his feet and switched on the bedside light. The clock indicated seven-fifteen. He'd overslept. Tyler had planned to leave for her grandmother's at seven.

His glance fell on a note pinned to her pillow, and he snatched it up.

"Tarzan," she wrote, "you were sleeping so soundly I couldn't bear to wake you. See you tomorrow at Gran's. I love you."

Everything was as they'd planned, but he couldn't shake the residual uneasiness caused by his dream. He reached for his jeans and was tugging them on when the phone rang.

"Mr. Slater," the caller said, "this is Deputy McSwain at the sheriff's office."

"Yes?" Jared made no effort to keep the impatience from his voice.

"The sheriff wonders if you'd come in to answer a few questions this morning."

Jared swore under his breath. "I'm going out of town—"

"This won't take long," McSwain interrupted. "Sheriff Tillett just wants to clear up some inconsistencies between your story and Stanwick's."

"There'll always be inconsistencies—the man's crazy!" Wedging the phone between his shoulder and ear, Jared tied his boots.

"This inconsistency's a whopper," the deputy insisted. "The doctor's seen Stanwick and states he's lucid now, and Stanwick claims *you* killed his wife and those other two women."

"What? That's bull—"

"And Stanwick's got a motel owner who corroborates that he was in Georgia the night Evelyn Granger died in Florida."

"Look, deputy, *I* didn't kill those women. And if Stanwick didn't, then who—"

The image of the scar-faced man from his dream flashed into his mind. The man in his dreams hadn't been Stanwick, and now the killer was after Tyler. The rest area Jared had dreamed about was between Asheville and Hickory, on the way to Chapel Hill. She'd had a fifteen-minute start on him, and he didn't have a second to spare.

"McSwain, I didn't kill anybody, but the man who did is headed east on the interstate." Jared described the rest area. "Call the highway patrol and have them meet me there."

"I wouldn't do that, Mr. Slater. If you don't come in voluntarily, the sheriff will have to bring you in for questioning."

"Fine. He can pick me up at the rest area. I'll need all the help I can get." *If I'm not already too late.* Jared slammed down the receiver, tucked his gun in his belt, and raced down the stairs.

Five minutes later, he maneuvered the speeding rental car around the mountain curves of the highway leading to Asheville, where he would pick up the interstate.

When he reached the outskirts of the city, going-to-work traffic slowed his pace, and he prayed that somewhere ahead of him, maybe on the eastern edge of Asheville, Tyler had been delayed as well.

As traffic retarded to a crawl, he pounded the steering wheel with his fists, while fear and frustration chewed at his gut. If Tyler was hurt, the fault would be his for not sending her away the moment he'd met her. God knew, he'd had enough warnings from his dreams.

As the traffic began to flow again, memories tortured him with their sweetness—his first glimpse of Tyler, standing on his doorstep like a snow queen with ice glazing the incredibly long lashes of her eyes and the cold nipping her porcelain cheeks to a delicate pink; her compassionate response when he'd revealed his terrible dreams; her plucky courage when the Volvo had wrecked; her triumph over her fear when he'd hurtled down the cliff face with her girded to his back. And sweetest of all, the glow of love in her eyes when he'd kissed her beneath the pulsing water of the shower.

He pressed the accelerator, heedless of the speed limit. If he didn't reach her in time, he didn't care what the law did to him.

His shoulders ached with tension, and he felt as if he'd been driving all day, but he'd only been on the road a little over two hours when he spied the exit sign for the rest area he'd seen in his dream.

Fear for Tyler almost incapacitated him as he drove into the parking area and spotted Tyler's car at the far end. Closer to him stood another vehicle—a battered green car, the killer's. No other cars or trucks were in sight, except those zooming by on the highway.

Jared screeched to a stop, jumped out and raced toward the rest rooms. Banging open the door to the women's room, he drew his gun.

"Tyler?" His voice echoed in the empty room.

He pivoted and dashed toward the men's room. It, too, was empty. Crashing out the rest room door, he darted into the parking area. The cars remained, but the killer and Tyler were nowhere in sight.

Anxiety almost suffocated him. He tried to think. The killer had a gun. If he'd used it to hijack another car, Jared might never find Tyler. Maybe it was already too late.

NOT LONG BEFORE, Tyler had lowered the car's visor against the glare of the morning sun that rose over the foothills. When she'd awakened, she'd longed to stay in bed with Jared and pass the morning in languid lovemaking, but he slept so soundly, she'd hesitated to wake him.

Instead, she'd stuck to their original plan, scribbled a note, and kissed him goodbye. Now the morning stretched fresh and calm ahead of her, as if in compensation for the terror of the past several days.

In a few hours, she would reach Chapel Hill and dazzle Gran with the news of her engagement. The old girl would be delighted. The tobacco-rich blue blood of the Slaters of Virginia would more than meet Gran's requirements for a suitable husband for her granddaughter, and when Jared arrived the next day, Gran couldn't help falling in love with him.

Tyler hummed along with the car radio. She'd been through hell with Jared, but that was over now. Life was good. She remembered when she'd kissed him goodbye—his fine, dark hair a stark contrast to the pillow linen, the muscles of his biceps bulging against the sheet. His strength had saved her from Stanwick's bullets. His love had added new meaning to her life.

She giggled. If she would fall off a cliff for him, she would follow him anywhere. Daydreams of their life together consumed her—long walks in the mountain woods, intimate evenings in front of the fire, passion-ate lovemaking in the loft bedroom, producing dark-haired, brown-eyed children.

A rest-area exit sign interrupted her reveries. She'd been driving two hours straight and needed to stretch her legs. A cup of vending-machine coffee wouldn't hurt, either.

She flipped on her turn signal and eased into the exit lane. A battered green car pulled in behind her.

After parking, she climbed out and breathed deeply of the fresh mountain air that was only faintly tainted by fumes from nearby traffic. Raucous cries of blue jays, fighting over picnic scraps, disrupted the morn-ing quiet. She grabbed her handbag and walked briskly toward the rest room.

A few minutes later, she exited, searching her purse for change for the vending machine. The arm around her neck and the gun barrel pressed to her temple came out of nowhere.

"Do as I tell you, lady," an angry voice snarled in her ear, "or I'll blow you away right where you're standing."

Disbelief melded with the fear that surged through her. Had she survived Stanwick's attacks only to die at the hand of a petty thief?

"Take my purse, my car, whatever you want." She forced the words through trembling lips and shoved her bag upward and over her shoulder.

"Shut up!" The man knocked the handbag into the hedge that lined the walk.

When he made no effort to retrieve it, her terror grew. The man was no thief. "What do you want?"

He tightened his arm around her neck, crushing her throat. "Your cooperation. Now, move!"

He shoved her ahead of him. She dug in her heels to impede their progress, but the man's strength overpowered her. He pushed her off the walk and around the side of the building, the cold, oily surface of the gun barrel pressed into her skin.

She considered screaming, but the only beings within hearing were the blue jays, still squawking over picnic spoils. She strained to view the rest-area entrance, hoping for an approaching vehicle, but the road remained deserted.

In spite of her resistance, her burly attacker managed to drag her easily across the open space to the fence that circled the perimeter.

At the fence, he eased his grasp but didn't withdraw the gun or allow her to see his face. "Climb over."

"No." She'd had enough training in self-defense to know never to enter a vehicle or a secluded area with an assailant—if she wanted to stay alive.

He burrowed the gun deep into the hollow of her cheek. "Over the fence or I kill you here."

"Then kill me. I'm not going into the woods with you." She stiffened her shoulders, waiting for the shot, wondering if she would feel it or hear the concussion of the blast.

She expected to die. What she didn't expect was to be tossed over the fence like a sack of potatoes. Her burgundy slacks caught on the top wire, breaking her fall. She felt them rip just before landing on her face in the humus of the forest floor. She pushed to her knees, spitting out leaves and dirt, ready to run.

A hand on her collar jerked her back. "You ain't going nowhere except where I tell you."

She attempted to turn, but the hand twisted her blouse to restrain her movements, dragged her to her feet, and shoved her through the underbrush, deeper into the trees.

Branches lashed her face as she crashed through dogwood and maple saplings, creating more and more distance between her and the rest area, her only source of help.

Her muscles, still sore from yesterday's exertion, screamed in protest, and she stumbled, falling face-down in the leaves. A knee between her shoulder blades prevented her from getting up, and horror rose like bile in her throat as hands fumbled at her waist, removing her belt from her slacks.

Dear God, he's going to rape me.

She struggled, kicking against the man's weight, but he caught her arms, pinned them behind her, and tied her hands with her belt. Hauling on her belt until she feared her arms would be wrenched from their sockets, he jerked her to her feet.

She gulped in air and screamed at the top of her lungs. "Help, somebody, help!"

"Scream all you want. We're so deep in the woods, ain't nobody going to hear you."

He twisted her to face him, but she couldn't bear to look at him. With a growl, he thrust her backward against a tree trunk, hooked his foot around her ankles, and yanked her feet from under her. Her bottom thudded against the ground, jarring her entire body. Her teeth nicked her tongue, and the metallic taste of blood filled her mouth.

Determined not to surrender to panic, she raised her head and caught her first full glimpse of her tormentor, a tall and bulky man whose faded clothes matched his features, giving him the washed-out appearance of an overexposed snapshot. Small eyes, so pale a blue they were almost colorless, assessed her from a face ripped from forehead to chin by a ragged scar. Ash-blond hair, wispy and thin, fell across his waxen forehead.

He towered over her and nudged her with his foot. "I don't mean you any harm—"

"You could have fooled me," she snapped. Every muscle in her body shrieked with pain.

He backed away until he came up against a tree trunk about six feet from where she sat, then slid to a sitting position with his gun pointed at her heart. "I just want you to do me a favor, then I'll let you go."

He's lying.

Deceit permeated his voice and his posture, and for a moment, she wished he would kill her and be done with it, rather than taunt her further with promises of release. But if she was destined to die, she wanted to know why.

"What kind of favor?" She prayed it wasn't sexual; that he would kill her quickly and cleanly without assaulting her first.

He reached into his faded denim jacket with his free hand, and extracted a folded sheet of paper from his shirt pocket. "Just sign this letter, Miss Harris."

Her head jerked up in surprise. "You know my name?"

"I know all I need to know about you." He licked his bottom lip, a gesture that made her shudder.

"But how—"

"That's not important now. Just sign this paper, and I'll let you go."

Instinct told her the moment he'd obtained her signature, she was a dead woman. Her only hope was that someone had arrived at the rest area and heard her screams. If she could stay alive long enough, maybe help would come. "I never sign anything I haven't read first."

"What are you, a lawyer?" He scowled. "God, I hate lawyers."

"I'm a librarian," she replied.

"I hate books, too."

Her heart pounded. "So, what does the paper say?"

He smoothed open the sheet against his knee. "Jared Slater—"

"Jared! How do you know Jared?"

He spat like a man with a bad taste in his mouth. "I wish to hell I didn't. I can't get the man out of my head. I know everything he's thinking—and he knows too much about me."

Understanding exploded like a bomb in her head. This man—not Pete Stanwick—had haunted Jared's dreams. "Stanwick *didn't* kill his wife!"

"That worked out good, didn't it?" His smile reeked of evil. "I made that bastard suffer. First, I killed his wife, and now everybody's thinking he did it."

Her hopes for survival plummeted. Her captor had killed before, so he wouldn't hesitate to kill her, too.

"Who are you?" she demanded.

"Don't you know by now?" He leaned back against the rough bark of the tree and narrowed his colorless eyes. "Ozzie Anderson was my father."

"You're Arnie?"

He nodded, looking pleased with himself.

"But your mother said you were in Alaska."

"Ma and I had this all worked out. She'd cover for me while I paid back the bastards that killed my daddy."

She shook her head in disbelief. "But Veronica Molinsky, Mary Stanwick and Evelyn Granger had nothing to do with your father's execution."

He shrugged. "But they were related to the men who did it. Ma and me wanted those men to suffer like we'd suffered all those years. Once I kill Slater, I'll finish off the others."

Fear for Jared renewed her determination to escape, to warn him. She pushed herself upright, hoping to seize a chance to bolt. "Why kill Jared? He knew nothing about your father."

Arnie's vicious cackle filled the stillness. "Yeah, but he knows too much about me. If I don't get him out of the way, they'll catch me before I can finish off the others."

She nodded toward the paper. "And that's what the note to Jared is about?"

"Yeah. It tells him when and where to meet me."

She arched her eyebrows. "Why would he do that?"

He grinned, exposing yellowed teeth. "Because you've signed it. Because it says the only way he'll ever see you alive again is to meet me."

Arnie Anderson was going to kill her anyway. She wouldn't help him trap Jared by signing his death warrant. "I'm not signing anything."

He heaved a sigh of frustration. "Have it your way."

"Then you'll let me go?" She clung to the glimmer of a chance.

"You?" he said with a mocking snort. "No way, lady."

Then he raised the blued barrel of the revolver and aimed it between her eyes.

Her last thought was of Jared and how much she loved him.

JARED SCANNED THE AREA, searching for any clue that Tyler might be close by. Sunlight glinted on a gold clasp in the hedge, and he withdrew a purse from the bushes. Tyler's wallet and keys were inside.

But where is she?

The killer could have forced her into another car and be miles away by now, or he could have dragged her into the surrounding woods. If Jared chose the wrong direction to search, he might never see Tyler alive again.

Desperate, he closed his eyes and concentrated. He'd never entered the killer's mind except in dreams, but now his only hope to save Tyler was to thrust himself into the killer's thoughts to discover where she was.

Sweat beaded his forehead as he blocked every sensation and focused on the killer, recalling every nuance of his face, every thought and black emotion. A whirling vortex of darkness sucked at him, drawing him deeper into nothingness. Fear clutched at his gut, breaking his concentration, but he swept it aside, homing in on the mind of the man who had kidnapped the woman he loved.

His body quavered with his efforts, his blood thundered in his ears, and his breath came in tortured gasps, until he wrested his perceptions away from himself and into the killer's head. Like a movie on a screen, a glimpse of the killer, propelling Tyler ahead of him and boosting her over a fence, flashed through Jared's mind.

Disoriented and queasy, with his legs threatening to fold beneath him, he opened his eyes. His attention flew to the fence, and he attempted to locate the spot where Tyler and the killer had crossed, but each segment of the long expanse looked alike. He sprinted to the western edge of the picnic area and followed the fence east, searching for some sign of their passage.

Midway, he spotted a scrap of burgundy cloth snagged on the fence directly behind the rest rooms. He grasped the top of the wire with both hands and started to clamber over. Behind him, tires squealed to a halt in the rest area.

"Jared Slater?" A uniformed highway patrolman exited his cruiser and raced toward him. "Stop right there!"

"Follow me!" Jared shouted over his shoulder. "There's no time to waste."

He vaulted over the fence and set off into the woods at a trot. The muffled curses of the patrolman followed him.

THE CONCUSSIVE BOOM of gunfire sounded in Tyler's ear as she flung herself to one side and rolled into the underbrush. She struggled to her feet. With her hands tied behind her back, the effort took forever, and she expected any minute to hear the roar of another shot and feel the bullet.

Behind her, Arnie grunted and cursed, but she didn't look back. Heading in the direction she hoped led to the rest area, she stumbled through the woods, striving to keep her balance without the use of her arms.

Arnie crashed through the foliage close behind.

Urging her aching legs faster, she ran, knowing her flight was futile, that a single bullet could bring her down, but refusing to make it easy for Arnie to kill her.

Her foot struck a root, sending her sprawling. Before she could rise, running footsteps pounded the ground beneath her ear, and she braced herself for the end.

Strong arms lifted her, and she struggled against them.

"Tyler, you're safe now."

The voice was Jared's. She had to be hallucinating in her fear. But when the powerful arms pressed her against a broad chest, and hands fumbled to untie the belt that bound her, she breathed deeply of Jared's unique scent—a masculine mixture of mountain air and sunshine that informed her she was truly safe.

When he had loosed her hands, she threw her arms around his neck. "Thank God. I was afraid I'd never see you again."

He clutched her to him, squeezing the air from her lungs, and she reveled in the security of his embrace.

Until she remembered Arnie.

She pushed away from Jared. "We have to run. Arnie Anderson's coming after me, and he has a gun."

Jared smiled a slow grin. "Not anymore."

She drew a sharp breath. "You didn't kill him?"

He flung an arm around her shoulder and accompanied her back the way she'd come. "No, but not because I didn't want to. Arnie's life was spared by the timely arrival of a highway patrolman."

"How did you find me?" She stopped and stared with astonishment. "How did you know I needed you?"

He shrugged. "Sometimes those blasted dreams come in handy."

When they reached the fence, he gave her a leg over, then leaped the barrier. In the parking area, lights of two highway patrol cars flashed, and uniformed officers placed a handcuffed Arnie into the back seat of the nearest cruiser.

Arnie glared at them before the door slammed, and Tyler glimpsed him long enough to view his swollen face and blackened eye.

"Did you do that?" she asked.

Jared nodded and tightened his arm around her shoulders. "It was either hit him or shoot him. He was ready to take another shot at you."

"What happens now?"

"We make a statement to the authorities."

She glanced at her watch. "Will I still have enough time to reach Gran's today?"

He shook his head.

She groaned. "Will the statements take that long?"

He turned her toward him and tipped her chin in his palm. His brown eyes blazed with emotion. "No, but going back to Lake Toxaway so I can pack, will. This time, I'm going with you."

She snuggled into his embrace, smiling at the thought of Gran's face when, out of the blue, she sprang her fiancé on the old girl.

Epilogue

A gentle breeze stirred the deep pink blossoms of crepe myrtles that encircled the wide porch, carrying the heady fragrance of roses from the nearby garden to the table where Tyler sat, addressing wedding invitations.

"Want some iced tea, dear?" Gran stepped through the French doors carrying an icy pitcher and tall glasses on a tray. She deposited her burden on the table and sat in the wicker rocking chair across from Tyler.

"Thanks. I'm almost finished here." Tyler slid the last of the heavy vellum cards into its matching envelope.

A worried crease joined the lines in the older woman's face. "I don't know what people will think, with you engaged *and* married in the space of six weeks."

Tyler accepted a glass of tea with one hand and grasped Gran's hand with the other. "They'll think I'm incredibly lucky to have found a man like Jared."

Gran nodded. "If they only knew. I still shudder when I think how close you came to being killed. Luck is the only thing that kept you alive during that entire ordeal."

"Not luck, Gran. Jared protected me."

Gran sighed. "He is a most remarkable man. Reminds me of your grandfather when he was young."

Tyler breathed a sigh of relief. Gran had just awarded Jared with her highest accolade. With Gran's approval won and Jared's reconciliation with his family accomplished, the wedding would be a happy event for everyone.

"But," Gran said, "there are still several things I don't understand."

"You know better than to ask me to explain love," Tyler said with a grin.

"Fiddlesticks." Gran withdrew a lace-edged handkerchief from the bodice of her lavender housedress and fanned her face. "I understand love well enough. It's why Peter Stanwick tried to kill Jared that I don't understand."

Tyler set the stack of wedding invitations aside. "Jared and I didn't understand, either—at first. But after we talked again with Robby, Pete's son, and interviewed the doctors who examined Pete, we discovered Pete believed Jared had killed his wife."

Gran's blue eyes widened. "Good heavens! Why would he think such a thing?"

Tyler shook her head sadly. "Mary's death caused Pete to have a mental breakdown. Since Jared, a total stranger, had appeared in town asking questions about Mary at the time she died, Pete was convinced Jared had killed her.''

''And now?''

''Pete's getting treatment. We're hoping a jury will go easy on him, under the circumstances.''

Gran's face wrinkled in distaste. ''I hope they show no mercy to that horrible Anderson creature.''

Tyler shivered, remembering. ''Not much chance of that. Between the ballistics matchup of Arnie's gun and the bullets that killed the three women, and Arnie's blood found at Veronica Molinsky's where he ripped his cheek open hiding in her rose arbor, he'll be put away for a long, long time.''

''Here's Jared now.'' Gran nodded toward a car pulling into the driveway and rose from her rocking chair. ''I'll bring another glass.''

She slipped into the house as Jared climbed out of his car. Tyler crossed to the porch steps to meet him. The sight of him made her heart pound and her pulse race, and when he drew her into his arms for a long, lingering kiss, she wondered if anyone ever died from sheer happiness.

He released her, and she crooked her arm in his and walked back to her chair. He sank into the rocker with a sigh.

''Were the tests rough?'' she asked.

He nodded, raking his fingers through his hair. ''Tedious. The parapsychology department at Duke

University is thorough. They have to be, in a field viewed with so much skepticism.''

She waited. He would tell her the results in his own time. The silence stretched between them, comfortable and intimate. One of the most fulfilling aspects of their relationship was their ability to communicate without words.

He nodded toward the invitations. ''Are those ready to mail?''

She grinned. ''I'll drop them off at the post office later this afternoon. Now's your last chance to back out before the die is cast.''

''Hmm.'' He scratched his chin. ''There's a thought.''

''Jared!''

With a mischievous grin, he grabbed her wrist and tugged her onto his lap. ''You know I'd marry you today if you'd forget this fancy wedding and run away with me.''

She nuzzled her face into his neck. ''Now, that would be a new experience—running away with you without cops and killers on our trail.''

His lips grazed her hair. ''We could hire Enrico and go back to the Birch and Bottle Inn.''

She sat back and glared at him with mock indignation. ''And forget the private honeymoon cottage in Bermuda? No way.''

He shrugged in resignation. ''You're right. Besides, I've grown fond of Gran and wouldn't want to disappoint her. What's a few more weeks? We'll have the rest of our lives together."

She settled contentedly into his arms.

"Tyler?"

The somberness of his tone made her sit upright and study his face. "Yes?"

"Are you sure you want to go through with this?"

"The big wedding?" Fear hammered at her heart.

He shook his head. "Marrying me."

"Of course, I'm sure. Why wouldn't I—"

"The test results. They were pretty conclusive." He turned away, avoiding her eyes as he stared across the deep side lawn.

"They won't change my mind." Her heart constricted at the pain in his eyes.

"You have to know that I'm *different*. My mind— it doesn't work like other people's." His flat, emotionless tone frightened her more than his expression.

She stroked his cheek with the back of her hand. "Tell me about it."

"They verified my psychic abilities, my heightened perceptions. That night in the emergency room, Arnie Anderson had just committed his first murder and was in a highly agitated state. When I suffered the aneurysm, my trauma produced a psychic conduit, connecting me to Anderson. That's how I shared his thoughts."

"But—" she drew back and met his gaze "—Arnie had nothing to do with sending the bomb, and you dreamed about that, too."

He nodded. "The tests also confirm I have strong powers of precognition."

"Precognition?"

"Clairvoyance. I can tell the future—some of the time. When I'm emotionally connected to someone or something." He grimaced as if the words left a bad taste in his mouth. "That makes me different."

She grasped his shoulders and met his gaze. "That makes you special. But I would marry you even *without* your extraordinary powers."

"If anyone's special, it's you." He clasped his fingers behind her neck and drew her head down, covering her mouth with his. She reveled in the scent of him filling her nostrils and savored the taste of him on her lips.

She lacked his precognition, but knew she would love this man forever.

When the kiss ended, she drew back, searching his face and finding her love reflected there.

"Have you had any more dreams?" she asked.

His face crinkled in the smile she adored. "Only good ones, and all about you."

She dipped her head for another kiss. "I promise to make all those dreams come true."

COMING NEXT MONTH

#381 RULE BREAKER by Cassie Miles
Lawman
Aviator Joe Rivers was hell-bent on discovering the real cause for his wife's fiery death in a plane crash. But he didn't expect to find himself falling in love again—and with a prime suspect. After all, it was sexy Bailey Fielding who helped pilot the craft in which Joe's wife was killed....

#382 SEE ME IN YOUR DREAMS by Patricia Rosemoor
The McKenna Legacy
Keelin McKenna dreamed through other people's eyes...victims' eyes. And when Keelin came to America in the hope of reuniting the McKenna clan, the dreams intensified. This time she couldn't ignore them—because somewhere out there was a father whose teenage daughter was missing. Tyler Leighton would come to rely on Keelin much more than she ever dreamed possible.

#383 EDEN'S BABY by Adrianne Lee
In the past, a woman had killed for Dr. David Coulter's love. Now the lovely Eden Prescott has pledged her love to David. But when she discovers her pregnancy, should Eden turn to the father of her baby...or will that make them all—her, David and the coming child—mere pawns in the game of a jealous stalker?

#384 MAN OF THE MIDNIGHT SUN by Jean Barrett
Mail Order Brides
Married to a stranger.... They're mail-order mates, and neither one is who they claim to be. Cold Alaskan nights roused a man's lust for a warm woman—and Cathryn matched Ben's every desire. He would enjoy sweet-talking her into divulging her deepest secrets...for she had slipped right into the ready-made role he had planned for her. And right into the trap he'd set....

AVAILABLE THIS MONTH:

Look for us on-line at: http://www.romance.net

Take 4 bestselling love stories FREE

Plus get a FREE surprise gift!

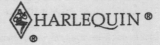

Sabrina   It Happened One Night
Working Girl   Pretty Woman
While You Were Sleeping

If you adore romantic comedies then have
we got the books for you!

Beginning in **August 1996** head to your
favorite retail outlet for
LOVE & LAUGHTER™,
a brand-new series with two books every
month capturing the lighter side of love.

You'll enjoy humorous love stories by favorite
authors and brand-new writers, including
JoAnn Ross, Lori Copeland, Jennifer Crusie,
Kasey Michaels, and many more!

As an added bonus—with the retail purchase,
of two new Love & Laughter books you can
receive a **free** copy of our fabulous
Love and Laughter collector's edition.

LOVE & LAUGHTER™—a natural
combination...always
romantic...always entertaining

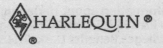

Look us up on-line at: http://www.romance.net

You're About to Become a *Privileged Woman*

Reap the rewards of fabulous free gifts and benefits with proofs-of-purchase from Harlequin and Silhouette books

Pages & Privileges™

It's our way of thanking you for buying our books at your favorite retail stores.

✂

PROOF OF PURCHASE
HI-PP159
Offer expires October 31, 1996

**Harlequin and Silhouette—
the most privileged readers in the world!**

For more information about Harlequin and Silhouette's PAGES & PRIVILEGES program call the Pages & Privileges Benefits Desk: 1-503-794-2499

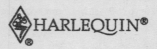

HARLEQUIN®

HI-PP159